Everything You've Heard Is True ☆
4/28/89

Len, you sweetiepie, good friend and super artist, all the love.
Frances

Johns Hopkins: Poetry and Fiction
John T. Irwin, General Editor

FICTION TITLES IN THE SERIES

Guy Davenport, *Da Vinci's Bicycle: Ten Stories*

Stephen Dixon, *Fourteen Stories*

Jack Matthews, *Dubious Persuasions*

Guy Davenport, *Tatlin!*

Joe Ashby Porter, *The Kentucky Stories*

Stephen Dixon, *Time to Go*

Jack Matthews, *Crazy Women*

Jean McGarry, *Airs of Providence*

Jack Matthews, *Ghostly Populations*

Jean McGarry, *The Very Rich Hours*

Steve Barthelme, *And He Tells the Little Horse the Whole Story*

Michael Martone, *Safety Patrol*

Jerry Klinkowitz, *"Short Season" and Other Stories*

James Boylan, *Remind Me to Murder You Later*

Frances Sherwood, *Everything You've Heard Is True*

☆ ☆ ☆ *Everything*

You've Heard Is True

SHORT STORIES BY

Frances Sherwood

The Johns Hopkins University Press
BALTIMORE AND LONDON

This book has been brought to publication with the generous assistance of the G. Harry Pouder Fund and the Albert Dowling Trust.

© 1989 Frances Sherwood
All rights reserved
Printed in the United States of America

The Johns Hopkins University Press, 701 West 40th Street, Baltimore, Maryland 21211
The Johns Hopkins Press Ltd., London

All of the stories in this volume appeared in the following periodicals, to whose editors grateful acknowledgment is made: *California Quarterly:* "The Red Fridge"; *Caribbean Writer:* "Everything You've Heard Is True"; *Confrontation:* "Me at the Gas Station"; *Greensboro Review:* "History"; *Kansas Quarterly:* "The Cat Woman and the Frog Prince"; *Literary Review:* "Lessons in Love"; *Massachusetts Review:* "Communiqué"; *Playgirl:* "Arrowheads"; *Seattle Review:* "Human Behavior"; *West Wind:* "Collect Calls"; and *Wind:* "Best Minds."

"History" also appears in *Prize Stories, 1989: The O. Henry Awards.*

The paper used in this publication meets the minimum requirements of American National Standard for Information Sciences—Permanence of Paper for Printed Library Materials, ANSI Z39.48–1984.

LIBRARY OF CONGRESS CATALOGING-IN-PUBLICATION DATA

Sherwood, Frances
   Everything you've heard is true.

   (Johns Hopkins, poetry and fiction)
   Contents: Arrowheads—The red fridge—Human behavior—[etc.]
   I. Title. II. Series.
PS3569.H454E94   1989   813'.54   88–46062
ISBN 0–8018–3823–1 (alk. paper)

To my brother Peter Sherwood

The heart is the toughest part of the body.
Tenderness is in the hands.

CAROLYN FORCHÉ

Contents ☆

Arrowheads	1
The Red Fridge	13
Human Behavior	17
Communiqué	27
Lessons in Love: A Memoir	34
Me at the Gas Station	43
History	55
Best Minds	69
The Cat Woman and the Frog Prince	80
Collect Calls	96
Everything You've Heard Is True	109

Everything You've Heard Is True ☆

Arrowheads ☆

Cats was an exception. Usually my taste in women is less exotic, for I am a man who favors plumpness, comfort, the delicately sloppy; that is, ladies with candy wrappers stuck to the bottom of their purses. Yes, the mothers.

I noticed Cats the first day of auto mechanics class. She moved among us with the cool grace of an adolescent boy. She flicked off the fan belt, undid screws as if born to machines. The second day of class we bumped heads under our instructor's car while inspecting tie rods. Changing the oil, we began to speak. I was nervous, actually, thinking that the car, jacked up by us students, might fall on my face. I hummed in the dark.

"It is a crime," Cats said, offering reassurance, "the way mechanics rip people off."

The oil glubbed down in ugly blops.

Afterward, I could see that loving Cats was a premeditated dip into hurt, yet she was something to be solved, not passed up. Warm and remote, enticing, forbidding, woman as mystery. Not, though, that I needed it, because I meet lots of nice women on my job. They bring their kids to see Rocky the Stuffed Raccoon. They press their lovely moon fingers to the warm plastic wall of the bees' house, which connects by tube to a hole in the wall, perfectly safe. Twice a day I put on the snake show (live) and press the planetarium buttons to magically project constellations in our small, concrete dome. Fixed patterns, I say, used for navigation since ancient man. Then I do the guided tour around the nature center. And often enough somebody stays for questions about the flora and fauna of Rock Creek Park. Are snakes vicious?

Is it fun being a park ranger? What, sir, is your sign? Snakes are cowards fearing feet, I answer. Life is fun, my dear. And my sign is Libra, meaning "balance," and I tip forward a little, tug my beard, slowly let my eyes slide snakes, ladders. I tell the lady how much I like her kids. She sighs in grateful relief, slices the French bread, passes the wine, and bites into her pear, looking coyly up into my waiting eyes. Yes, a picnic. Yes, I understand. I understand everything.

Cats's eyes were tawny, lighter than her skin. She wore her coarse black hair in a thick braid down her back. Her mouth thin, the smile closed as if holding back for later. Her nose was large, regal. Indian, but more brave than squaw in her jeans and wrinkled flannel shirt with mother-of-pearl snap cowboy buttons. She was free of turquoise, beads of any kind.

After the first week of class when everyone else was still on oil change and we had moved on to tune-up, I asked her name.

"My name is Cats, from Catherine."

"Want to go for a drink after class?"

"Don't drink firewater," she answered, busy rubbing a dirty spark plug.

"Wise of you. Do you smoke?"

"Sometimes, on occasion."

"Treaties?"

"Exactly."

"How about food?"

"I don't have any money today." She wiped her hand on her shirt, gave me a defiant smile.

"My treat," I replied.

"You don't know me," she said studying the radiator, "and you're treating?"

"Yep."

"What is the catch?"

"No catch, I'm independently wealthy."

Though both of us were smudged with grease, I drove her to a classy place in downtown Washington which specialized in vegetarian cuisine and sitar music.

"Boy," she said, chewing the end of her braid, "this is really nice."

I shrugged.

"But I better let you know before the food that I have kids."

"I know."

"How?"

"I'm an expert."

"I'm divorced, too."

"Divorced is fine."

"My husband lives with me. My ex, that is."

"Oh, an open divorce?"

"In a way." She moved back in her chair, took a worried sip of water.

"Sounds heavy."

"It is."

"I see." Of course, I didn't see, but the waiter appeared, Cats ordered the one meat dish on the menu, and when it arrived she held her head close to the plate, taking small, quick bites. Finished way before me, she wiped her whiskers clean (she had a soft, black mustache that she had the grace not to bleach), and, focusing on my scar from a youthful encounter with an older woman and her irate husband, Cats began the story of her life.

"We married young. I was a biology student. I dreamed of being kind of a naturalist out in the woods, gathering things. Gabriel is a potter. It takes time to get established in art. Not like accounting. God, you have such blue eyes, like quarry water. The long hair, the beard, too. Are you hiding yourself in it?" She took a breath. "Anyway, Gabriel and I were sitting there one day getting to be thirty when we realized that we had spent our whole adult life in the state of holy matrimony. Boy, was it scary."

"Why?"

"It was that we had never faced anything. Who we were. When I looked in the mirror, I saw Gabriel, and, believe me, we are not anything alike."

"Oh."

"The first thing after the divorce, I put in an answering machine, so not to miss a call. I anticipated a mob, a rush, dates, proposals, but after a while I knew nobody would call."

She laughed. I didn't. Truly, I could not imagine her that eager.

"It didn't work out; maybe I, we, were too old. When we got back though, to each other, something was gone. The marriage was gone, but Gabriel stayed anyway. It is convenient. He lives at my house."

"Platonically?" I like to get my facts straight at least.

"I'm not good at Platonic," she said.

"Who is?"

"We are not in love, you know, lovers, like that."

Well, it sounded too strange even for me. Kids I can deal with. But leftover husbands? Even with a real divorce there is a lingering sense of property complete with fence, which is why I like forest. Live and let live and, in this case, let alone. However, driving home, Cats opened her mouth and more life spilled out, swirling around me like a flood. I began to feel engulfed, then part of it.

Cats McPherson drew blood for a living. Lab technician, she demonstrated with a tiny sucking sound.

Her kids, Tony and Tania, were fifteen and eleven, respectively.

Yes, she was mostly Indian, but from a tribe other Indians called Women because they didn't fight, were known to cry before the Trail of Tears. The Lenni Lenape were driven to the reservation in Oklahoma like cattle, she said, and there obliterated by liquor, the white man's disease. She hissed this with her lips drawn back.

"I escaped," she said glumly. Because some of her ancestors were white. "But there is no winning, none at all."

Her husband, Gabriel, came from Scottish coal miners. Both of them, she said, were Pennsylvania Poor. And in the narrative, she kept returning to him, the worker in clay, her husband, so that I knew theirs was a relationship that was neither open nor closed but rather always in question. I couldn't help thinking of a great saw-jawed bear trap I had seen once. It opened to release its prey, but not without mangling and crippling.

"What is your name?" she finally asked, putting her light, brown hand on my sleeve.

"Harry. My name is Harry."

"You know, Harry, it is weird, but as I tell you my troubles I feel happy. Hey, we're here, stop."

And I braked abruptly in front of a huge misshapen piece of gingerbread on a side street in Takoma Park.

"I add on," she explained of the house. A Dodge lay low under some pines. "Come on in."

"Ah, Cats, is your husband home?"

"No problem, Harry. No problem at all."

She pulled me through the door and down an old-fashioned hall with wallpaper and lights like candles in brassy holders fixed to the wall. We emerged into a living room filled with couches and worn rugs. On one couch was a huge hump of a man with a sleeping bag thrown over his back.

"Gabriel," she whispered, pointing needlessly.

He looked like an angel, an angelic, burly sheepdog with blond, almost white bangs covering his head like shingles.

"Think maybe I'd better run along." I whispered.

"He doesn't care."

And she pulled me through the living room and on down another hallway.

"Tony," she said softly, opening a door. Her son had decorated his room with Jimi Hendrix in all stages of agony, and the head on the pillow was bordered with rows of tiny braids. They looked like sleek, fat worms.

"Tony is trying for an Afro, but it comes out Indian."

Tania in the next room was striving for a Goldilocks. There were shelves and shelves of bears. Two were having late-night tea at a table.

"You have freaky kids," I told Cats as we continued on.

"I know," she said proudly.

Her room was a mattress on the floor with a great patchwork quilt. The squares looked like a view from an airplane—brown, neat, yellow, rusty, lots of green. On a box near the bed lay a row of black clay pipes.

"My peace pipes, Harry."

An easel in the corner held a mirror.

"You want to see the bathroom?"

"Not particularly."

But she pulled me on through the maze. The bathroom was a huge room. The cold, white fixtures, illuminated by the moon through an uncurtained window, startled me. The old, claw-footed tub, the toilet, all that loopy white seemed to grow up out of the tiled hexagons of the floor like enchanted mushrooms in a midnight forest.

"This is the only door that locks," she said, locking the door behind us.

"Cats. . . ." I started to shiver.

"Pull off my boots, Harry," and she hitched herself up on the sink.

"Cats. . . ." I pulled off her boots.

She slid off the sink and quickly unwrapped the leather skirt she was wearing, stood still for a minute, stretched and dropped her underpants, kicking them under the sink.

"Alleyoop," she said, hitching herself back on the sink. "This thing better not collapse on us."

"Cats, I think . . ."

"What's the matter, Harry, cold feet?" She looked down. "Oh my skirt." With one tug, she unsnapped the whole thing, flung it into the tub.

"Cats, what if somebody wakes up?"

"I have to throw water on them in the morning, okay?" She took my face in the two hands. "Mind at ease?"

I was nervous as hell, actually, but there in the moonlight, perched on the sink, well. . . . Cats was solid brown, her skin elastically tight on her bones. There were no bikini triangles, nothing frivolous, superficial. It was all serious. I am talking about her body, about her.

"I like you, Cats. I like you so much, but . . ."

"But what?"

"Dear, you seem to have so many problems. I mean, further complications, Cats, I don't want to hurt you."

"Harry," she breathed softly in my ear, "this will be my medicine. You be my medicine man."

☆ Many moons ago people sang and danced for rain, for warmth, for buffalo. The people crisscrossed the dry, rustling plains barechested, hair full of feathers.

"Cats."

"Shh, I know."

"Cats."

I carried the knowledge of her like a charm around my neck.

"Cats."

And all that fall, I met her every weekday after work. Then we'd drive over to pick up Gabriel and the kids at the house. The idea of Gabriel, former husband, present boarder, distressed me at first, but, meeting him, I found a brotherly, harmless sort, more child than man and certainly in no way a rival. Spending the day in the basement at the potter's wheel, he emerged gray with clay.

"Harry, hi, how are you? A beer?"

It was always as if he hadn't seen me in years, simply delighted, my goodness. Old chums. While I rocked in the kitchen rocking chair under the drying herbs, pots and spoons, strings of ancient Christmas tinsel, Gabriel showered. Out of politeness, it seemed, he let me dry him, asked please would I fluff up all the blond fur matted to his back. Tony and Tania got to rub his legs. Tania combed him down. Oh, Gabriel McPherson was the big Scandinavian rug, the Big Daddy Bear, but not with the gruff "Who has been eating my porridge?" Clean, bushy, he sat down in his towel, slowly smoked. Only with gentle urging would he hold up his arms for the long sleeves of his shirt. Tony drew on the pants, did the buckle for his father. In the Safeway, Gabriel trailed after us, picking out the cookies. I did vegetables, fruit, and Cats did the meat, while the kids read magazines at the checkstand. After dinner, we sometimes went to the movies, shows, lectures on black holes, bagpipe demos on the Mall. We popped popcorn in the fireplace, did all that family stuff. Then about nine, Tony tucked in with Motown, Tania dreaming of her furry, prehuman planet, and Gabriel obligingly sacked out under his sleeping bag, Cats and I would sneak to the bathroom, the kitchen, the car, sometimes my place. But we never, never went to her room. Too conjugal, she joked of her bed. It was a bad joke, it turned out, for we never quite developed that intimacy which comes of actually sleeping together, waking up together, having breakfast, crumbs and the paper, in bed; that is, there were no weekends.

"Weekends are out, Harry. No discussion. I respect your privacy."

She did indeed. No questions about parents, college major, old love, new hate, nasty habits. There was none of that neurotic digging so characteristic of affairs (you show me yours, I'll show you mine), and I should have welcomed the change.

But one Saturday, the park too snowed-in for traffic, Nature Center closed, I didn't have to go to work and instead, breaking the weekend taboo, drove over to Cats's. Slipping and skidding the whole way, I got to her door, sensed something. The air was stale, stagnant. There were no sounds.

"Anybody home?" I called out, meeting Gabriel half-lotus on the rug. "Hey, where is everybody?" He stared straight ahead, said nothing.

I went into Tony's room. He, too, was sitting, staring. No music blared from his tapes.

"Where is your mom?"

"Cats?" I opened her door, and there she was, in bed, flat on her back, lids open. Her eyes registered no recognition and her limbs were dead in my hands. I rushed back to the living room.

"Gabriel, what is this, meditation hour? What the fuck is going on?"

"It's her head," Gabriel finally answered wearily.

"Migraines?"

"Cats doesn't get up on the weekends, Harry."

"The whole weekend?"

He nodded.

"How long has this been going on?"

"I've been with Cats about fifteen years, a little longer."

"And you never took her to the doctor about it?"

"I took her."

"What did he say?"

"She put Cats in the hospital for the weekend, but by Monday Cats wanted out. It lasts just the weekend. Some people get drunk, Harry."

"Sure, and they are crazy, too. Do you do anything else?"

"Everything I could think of." He stood up, put his hands in his pockets, started to pace. "Like, for instance, Harry, we had Tony, got married, had Tania, got divorced. We went on trips, Harry, came home, made fudge, ate it, got high, stayed straight. I talked to her. I asked her what the matter was, and you know what she told me? She said, Harry, that I didn't love her enough. Love her enough? Listen, Harry, I love that woman so damn much it's killing me."

He stopped, exhausted with the effort of so many words, collapsed back on the sofa. He looked at me skeptically, wiped a tear that was sliding into his beard.

"At least I have my art," he concluded.

"Yes," I agreed sadly, patting his knee, "at least you have your art."

Gabriel's art was piled in the basement, back from the kiln, glazed, finished, unshown. Pitchers, cups, bowls rose in stacks like ancient ruins, dusty artifacts of a dead culture. But he loved Cats. Of course. I was blind. And the divorce took on new dimensions, grew petals, horns.

Going back to her room, I took off my clothes, got in bed with her. I tried to cuddle, but it felt like assaulting a stone. She wasn't asleep, yet she was inaccessible. Her eyes open, I wondered what she was seeing. Perhaps she took something from her lab that produced an interior picture gallery of exploding colors, ethereal visions. Was she merely playing dead while her spirit roamed, exploring some ancestral landscape? Were the chemicals manufactured from within, the catatonia homemade? I didn't know, couldn't ask and, after a while, dozed off beside her. Once, looking up from the bed, I realized it was night. The second time I woke up I could see stars. That scared me, so with purpose I got up, dressed, brushed my teeth with my finger, splashed cold water on my face. Loudly, my steps exaggerated, I went into the kitchen, opened drawers, rattled dishes. I fried up a big bunch of potatoes and onions, corn fritters, apples.

"Come and get it," I hollered.

Tony set the table and I turned on the radio to a peppy Spanish station. "*Mis amigos, mis amigas, esta es neuva.*" Tania cleared, Gabriel washed, "*Mi amor,*" the radio sang sadly into the night.

However, Monday after work, Cats greeted me upright in her starched lab coat, stiff jeans, boots saddle-soaped to a fine sheen.

"Cats, we have to get something settled."

We had finished dinner, were out, alone in the quietest place in town: the Christian Science Reading Room.

"We have to get something straight."

She sat up straighter.

"I'm not kidding."

She smiled.

"I'm serious."

She scowled clouds.

"Do you remember the weekend?" I was having trouble remembering myself.

"Weekends are bad news, Harry."

"The worst. No news."

She took my hand, bit my thumb.

"You can't spend so much of your life as a zombie."

"The only good Indian is a dead Indian, or haven't you heard."

"Oh, Cats, I'm not playing hide-and-seek with you."

"Cowboys and Indians?"

"Listen to me. You have to get out of that."

She put her hand under the table, touched me.

"This is no solution, Cats."

"No problem, Harry, no problem."

So I dropped it for the time, let it go, but when I took her home, thought of her room, it came back.

"You have that look in your eye again, Harry."

We were in the kitchen. She was making me some red zinger. The herbs hanging down from the rafters were pungent as the woods.

"Let me play you my favorite song. It's really Tania's record from a collection called *Songs to Grow By*."

She brought the little child's player in, put on the record.

You can wear my mommy's hat,
You can wear my daddy's shoes,
You can do this and that, but
Don't you push me down.
Don't you, don't you,
Don't you push me down.

"Okie music, Harry, dustbowl song."

"But, Cats, I'm trying to lift you up. Trust me. I love you."

She looked at me with the greatest suspicion, started to gnaw her braid.

"I love you," I said again, and I was about to say that I would do anything for her, take her away, anything, when I remembered that she must have heard it all before and that the author was snoozing away in the living room. I looked at her. She had bit her lip, so it was bleeding and she was sucking it. I saw that, and then, looking up, I thought I saw something else, two things. Up there in all the dusty bay leaves hanging over the stove, amid the cooking gear, was a clump of dried mushrooms, big buttons, and also the hinges of a trap strung and set, its teeth glinting sharp, big enough for a bear.

"When I was in the hospital," she was saying, like an ordinary woman, "out on the terrace that was all wired in so we couldn't jump, they strung up a punching bag. No matches allowed, little glowing circles in the wall for cigarettes. So many precautions, it seemed indecent not to try a little self-destruction. Then the doctors came around. My doctor told the students, pointing at me as if I didn't have eyes to see, 'She's hallucinating.' Harry, I wasn't hallucinating up to that point."

"My dear," I took her hand, pressed it to my mouth, that lovely, cool brown hand.

"I told you not to come on weekends."

"Please."

"In the hospital, that punching bag on the terrace was for our aggressions, but we all used to go out and hug it."

"You want a hug? Come, let me hug you."

But the weekends went on, nothing settled.

Sometimes I just sat there by her bed, hoping to inspire resurrection by mere presence and loyalty. There seemed something sacred about her state, so I dared not interfere or intrude. It reminded me of a movie I had seen once about the Donner Pass. White men had trespassed through an Indian burial ground, and that had been enough to bring down a curse on the whole party. The Indian bodies had been placed on platforms in trees for vultures to pick clean, and it was eerie. There was that same sense of violation and taboo with Cats's craziness.

Sometimes I crooned a soft lullaby. "Last of the Lenni Lenape," I sang, "Do you remember the good days, the harvest days, the days of our love, that we are lovers which is all, which is enough." And sometimes it worked. One Sunday night, as I was sitting in the kitchen, having given up, she appeared in the doorway ghostly in her white nightgown, a faint smile on her drawn face. I tempted her out the door, with Tania and Tony following with her slippers, coat. They crowded quietly into the backseat of the car with their father, and we slowly rolled down the hill, picked up speed and headed toward Rockville, where they have the Toboggan Slide. In the lodge, sitting by the big fireplace on stumps, we had hot chocolate. In the flickering light, Cats sparkled. Tony looked at me as if I were Stevie Wonder. Tania petted me. Gabriel purred. And I had the foolish belief that Cats and I would hike the Appalachian Trail, go west, cross frontiers.

That never happened.

Getting Cats out of bed was a full weekend's work, a labor I grew tired of in two month's time. What can I say? Pathology is for real doctors? Addiction is in the blood? That I was no magician? Did it matter? Or was it merely that if you know somebody long enough they turn, revealing all seasons, an unsunned side? Was Cats's problem a long-time cultural grief or a modern inability to cope? Perhaps it was simple exhaustion. God, I didn't know.

What happened is this: Her bleak vision during those weekend days began to color everything, seeping into the week like spilled ink. The weight pressed down on me, and the fact that Cats was beautiful, wonderful, even that I loved her became irrelevant. During the week we made love as before, in corner places, but desperately locking limbs, grabbing, pulling, hurting each other. We could not deny the inevitable. Other women who for seven months had only been blurs gained focus. The Nature Walks started up with the first green of spring. Are snakes dangerous? Where is the poison oak? My sign is Libra, I answer. Means "balanced," I tease. Yet at the last minute there is my hallucination—Cats in war paint, lurking, bow and arrow poised for the kill.

It didn't work out that way. Late one Sunday night, heavy with guilt over staying away the whole weekend, I decided to drive over, peek in. Of course, the house was quiet—I expected that—but the hour was long past Gabriel's bedtime and he was not on the couch. Sick with premonition, I opened Cats's door, and I knew immediately what I was going to see, what I should have known at the beginning, but it was too late and the shock was none the less.

On that bed, that conjugal bed, he was working over his wife like a stonecutter chipping off flints. Her legs were up around him and she was making those little gasping rabbit sounds I knew so well. For a moment it was as if the kaleidoscope I was looking through had broken in my eye, the slivered pieces sticking straight in. And then the stinging was washed away, and, through the warm, salty veil, I saw Gabriel's buttery behind flap like soft wings around the flame, the mouth.

"Harry," Cats gasped, her eyes rolling back, her head at a jut.

Gabriel fell on her with a great shudder, and slowly they pulled the quilt over their bodies, over their heads, as if drawing the curtain on the final act of a sad, inevitable play. I backed out and the quilt became again, as on the first night, a scene from an airplane. I saw patches of pasture, yellow fields, the blue square of a lake from a great distances, for I felt myself floating. From a great distance, I could make out a man and a woman, kin obviously, husband and wife. That image, in time, diminished even further, so Cats, Gabriel, were only arrows—tiny spots of pain marking a point in time.

The Red Fridge ☆

The first fridge on the block belong to Mable next-door. She carry on as if it the first fridge on the whole island of Trinidad. But for sure the governor, he had one, maybe two, and the Americans on the base, they not without the comforts. Nineteen-fifty and electricity is discovered even in Arima, though what those country people want with light bulb, I don't know.

Mable DeContesta, then, act like Princess Margaret, Port-of-Spain, sitting at her window, her two big breasts hanging over the ledge like they black-ripe avocados in a dress, and her red fridge position just so. Only person not seeing it as he pass by in front is Mr. Singh, blind since a baby. But Mable describe it to him, including the legs, the handle, everything, a hour of talk. First time I go by since she got it, I hear her voice calling me.

"Good morning, Mrs. Rama." She talking sweet-sweet like the queen come for tea or something.

"Notice my new appliance?" Oh boy, that girl put on style for so.

"Sure I notice," I answer. "It right there, almost falling out of your window and red is what I call a noticeable color."

The red, let me tell you, was bright. It so red, it hurt.

"Theos," that what she call Theophilus, the poor man. "Theos, he give me for our anniversary. Should lasts till our Golden Jubilee."

Whether Theos make it so long is another question, but I quiet.

"Does it work, Mable?" That's important in a refrigerator. You don't want your fridge to be a coal pot, or your coal pot be a block of ice. Each thing got its job.

"Sure it work, you think I have appliance in my house and it not work? What the point?"

"Just asking," I say, "but you must excuse me." I give her impression I have more important to do than talk about some old machine. I have my children to see after, my husband, tea for the evening, school clothes to set out for the next day.

"Got to lift my wings," she say, taking her two chests in her hands and moving them off the ledge, "hoist my ass and see about Theos's dinner."

It nearly five and she getting off the box at her window for the first time all day except for latrine business. Nearly five and only then she sending Theos, Jr., off to buy some machine bread. She a criminal woman, the way she look after her family. Even before her fridge, she at the window all day.

I talk it over with my husband. What we can't understand is why some people are so foolish. Two rooms, ten children, and then they go out to buy American fridge. What they want with such a thing when you can get fresh every day at the market is the mystery. What my husband wonders is where they all sleep. That is the real puzzle. Twelve people and one old bed. Sometimes we think of the DeContestas all in one pile, child on top of child, Mable the biggest on top.

And if Mable get a notion in the night for making more, the whole turns into a chugging train going into the mountains.

Maybe take turns, is what my husband say. More reasonable than a pile when you start to think of that bed, which is feeble like the orphans who sewed it over at the Poorhouse. But then, the girls starting to sleep out at the time of the fridge. Not that they were, are, or even would be anything I'd call raving beauties.

And Theos, I forgot to say at beginning, he work upholstery. All day he at the shop stitching couch and so, while Mable rest herself on the box at the window. Once a year at Christmas they all put on shoe and march to church. It a sight, I'm telling you.

We find out the truth of the fridge when Theos die one day. All men got to die, say the priest, to be reborn again like Christ who save us, but Theophilus, I say, got to die sooner than most. Before his time, he went down to come up. And that for reasons starting with for one, he hardly got a good meal, for two, hardly a good rest, and for last, paying off that red fridge killed him to the ground. After a while he couldn't go to the shop anymore and just stay on the bed coughing through the whole day.

"Have you seen my new fridge?" goes on Mable meantime, the coughs getting weaker and weaker, the man going.

He die. Sure he die. Die fast. If you feed them right, they can hang on, but Theophilus DeContesta might as well starve to death, the food passing between his lips. No Golden Jubilee for him. I go over to pay my respects, as it proper. Two boards on the floor I find.

"No use taking up bed when you dead," explain Mable.

At least the man have on a pair of clean drawers and white shirt. Two shillings are set in his eyes. The kids outside playing monkey as usual, no respect for their dead Daddy. Me, oh Lord, how I hate to see the dead, but duty is duty. I there sitting with the body on the one chair. I there for a good little time when Mable forgetting I there, she opens her fridge. Hanging there inside fridge on a hanger is Theos's wedding suit.

"Your fridge a closet, Mable?" Now I the queen.

"Oh," she say, "just put it there for cooling. Cold helps keep the body fresh and smelling nice. Like to offer you a glass of ice water, Mrs. Rama, but, considering the suit, I don't make ice today."

"I see." I do see, but decide not to rub it in. The girl just lose a husband and by the looks of it, of everything including that make-believe fridge, that's the last husband she is ever going to get.

Well, the next item in the arrangements is that she cannot find a tie for him to wear with the suit. Mable send her old mother, Jay-Jay Alvarez, down the street after a tie to borrow from the neighbors. Just to borrow, she suppose to say. Just to borrow? If you let your tie go down into the grave, are you going to see it again? First off, it's bad luck to send something underground, you soon to follow, and if you send it with a man who never had a lucky day after his wedding, you tempting trouble double. Naturally, then, Jay-Jay come back puffing, empty-hand.

"One thing I know," Mable say to me, "is I am not going out to the store and wastes money on a new tie."

We sit around scratching our brains for a while, but one thing I know is that I am not going to take no tie off my husband's nail. After a time, they realize my position, and Jay-Jay go out in the back and bring in a rag from the line. They sponge it down with white bleach (my bleach, just to borrow) and knot it around his skinny neck.

"You know, Mrs. Rama," Mable say to me when she done, "Theos just smile at me. He proud he looking so nice."

I'm telling you. The next thing she throwing herself down, kissing that dead face. Oh God, the sight revolting. I hate to see people kissing up the corpses, no matter how good they looking.

Well, so it over. They bury the man. And Mable continue to sit at her window, the fridge set just so behind her. Carnival coming and with the activity picking up on the street, she more in her glory than ever. All day long it is, "Have you seen my new fridge?" and so forth. Just this morning, she bothering me to stop by and visit. But I have to tell her that I must work on my costume for Carnival.

"Ah, so you playing *mass* again this year, Mrs. Rama?"

I know she would like to play, too, but what can she wear with all her money going into appliance?

"Yes, I playing *mass*," I answer matter-of-fact.

"What are you going to be, Mrs. Rama, what are you going to play?"

"Queen, as usual."

Human Behavior ☆

I met Milo at the Nuthouse, a beer and pool place in Palo Alto, California, in 1975. The Nuthouse featured honky-tonk and country, Stanford kids acting tattered in jeans and Texas accents. The tone suited my mood at the time, and on paydays I usually dropped in for a beer or two. Recently separated from my husband of eight years, I was trying to act alive, go through the motions. When Milo came up to my booth, I hadn't talked to a man in six months, not since my last fight with Sam.

When I left Sam I had to move in with my mother in her "retirement" trailer in Half Moon Bay, and after I got my job, with a small loan, I was able to take an apartment in Mountain View. It was in a white stucco building with plastic foliage in the window boxes. Recovering from the high, authentic art that was life with Sam, I found the tackiness of Villa Allegra comforting.

But looking for a job, I had vague illusions of doing something "interesting," meaning working in a museum guiding tours or writing for an avant-garde art magazine. I had actually studied art history for two dedicated years until becoming an artist's wife. But it seemed that even boring typing jobs were beyond my reach, my fingers freezing up on typing tests, and so I ended up shifting books in the basement of the Stanford Primate Center, all the monkey books transferring from the main library on campus up to the hill. Across from the Primate Center was the linear accelerator, a long concrete tunnel for smashing atoms and discovering some secrets of the universe.

The night I met Milo I noticed him watching me from his table for a good twenty minutes. Then he got up, scooped a handful of peanuts from the big barrel, came over. He was wearing a cap and vest, outdated full pants with little pleats at the waist.

"You a student?" He sat down without invitation.

"A worker." I inched over. He smelled like olives.

"Me, too." He looked pleased with my answer. "Me, I'm through with academic bullshit." And with that, he settled in.

"Almost got my Ph.D.," he confided, his voice lecture-loud, and pool players, naturally curious, stopped playing pool. Linda Ronstadt was blaring in the background: "You're no good, no good, baby, you're no good."

"See, I went to those conventions, hiring halls. Twenty openings and hundreds, hundreds, honey, of applicants, and all eating crackers in their hotel rooms in their underwear to save money and the crease in their suits. Meantime back downstairs, the big boss giving out the jobs slugging down Chivas Regal, and the résumés of the interviewees falling like snow to the floor. And they are stepping on them. What can I say, I rest my case. And that's economics, darling, one of the better fields."

I didn't doubt it for a minute.

"Actually, I lost my faith." He leaned forward, stroked his Zapata mustache meaningfully. "I studied profit maximization, supply and demand, utility, trade, money, macro, micro, all the magic words. It's a religion. You got to believe the dogma, those first axioms, or you can't go on. Like take the basic assumption that man is rational. Man is not rational, or woman either. Humans are not rational. You know that. I know that. Man is mad, chaotic, full of contradictions."

"We have habits, patterns," I cautiously ventured.

"Based on instinct or some crazy nonsense, not free will."

I smiled my elusive smile. It was something I had practiced in high school and hadn't used in years, but he seemed to respond to it.

"Hey, you want to go to the movies." He patted my hand like a pal.

Driving down the palm-lined entrance to Stanford in the moonlight, he told me he was a tree surgeon. I told him I was separated, unhinged. My nerves seemed to jangle as the tree-cutting paraphernalia in the back of his trunk jiggled and bounced. His dog, Max, confined to the back, looked in at the window as if I had stolen his place. Milo told me he wanted to open a plant store. In the close cab of the truck, he smelled like bay leaves. Max bared his teeth. I told Milo my ex-husband was an artist, a successful one. Milo replied that those were the worst kind. In the movie, *The Bicycle Thief*, he cried copiously and continuously, using the empty sleeve of my sweater to wipe his tears. Walking from the Business School Auditorium, where the movie was held, to the coffee house on the other side of campus, he told me he had seen that particular movie ten times and that everybody in the movie was real, not actresses and actors, but real people who you would see on the streets of Italy any day of the week, of course during that time.

"That's what I like about you, Clair. You look ethereal, but really, you are so real. See, I believe that long-run we come to nothing, so it is short-run that counts. Me, I'm down-to-earth."

I was glad to hear that and also glad to see the lights of the coffee house. Inside, it was packed with students in their bulky down jackets. The rock band, heavy metal, was out taking five, and Keith Jarrett was on the record player. The expresso machine was on the blink, so we had American coffee. Milo had pumpkin cake and I had baklava. I removed the sweet thin flakes of pastry one by one to make it last.

"You're a very sexy girl," Milo said.

"Woman," I corrected.

"Thin women have nerves close to the surface," he said.

"Oh?"

Then an announcement was made that the rock band had a misunderstanding and would not be back after their break.

"Everyone and their little ego," Milo said. "I'm glad you're not on that trip."

I thought I did have an ego, but I let the remark go. Mainly, I did not want to spoil the occasion—that is, a man sitting across from me showing a little interest, any interest. But Max, waiting outside for us, scratched at the glass.

"Clair," Milo said. "Clair, you are nice. I really like you. We have to see more of each other. You think?"

"Oh yes," was my eager answer. Yes, indeed.

Between Sam and Milo, I brushed my teeth ten times a day. Also I washed my wispy hair until it fell out in clumps. I read lots of junky books and the evening and morning newspapers. I went to garage sales and, if all else failed, wrote letters to Sam which I never sent. My medicine cabinet was filled with those desperate jottings, and roaches had laid eggs between the thin sheets, leaving a trail of antique tracks.

December 5, 1975

Dear Sam,

The library is in the basement of a Primate Center. We in the library are not permitted to see the monkeys (only behavioral scientists), but we can hear them pacing. They say that monkeys carry around their dead babies in their arms for days, won't let go. They don't take loss well. And they can predict earthquakes, like arthritics before a storm. I consult my bones like tea leaves at the bottom of a cup, but they tell me nothing about the future.

    I spent Christmas with my mother in her trailer. We had cornish hens and with her macrame sculptures hanging down everywhere over our food and fringing the TV set, I felt like I was in the Amazon Rain Forest eating something wild.

January 8, 1976

Dear Sam,

Well, I made it through Christmas. It was only a little harder than Sundays. But, you know, monkeys sit on chairs, ring for food, wear dresses, carry on in a generally human way. The other day, a cat wandered into one of the cages and I understand the monkey of the house, I think Coco, tried to make the cat sit in a chair and learn a lesson.

In those days I slept with the light on, yet I had a recurring nightmare. I was locked in a tower, and, when I looked down, I could see a group of gorillas going for a walk. It was dark and chilly, and the gorillas wore little capes that flapped in the wind. In that doubtful light, the shadowy figures with the hulking shoulders gave the impression of a little platoon of supermen. Once, after the nightmare, I phoned Milo. It was two o'clock but he answered the phone brightly. And that day he met me at work during my lunch hour. He was wearing his tree boots, and his flannel shirt bore splinters. We went out in the wood overlooking the linear accelerator.

    "Once I had a dream that I was a cannonball lady shooting out of the accelerator. I landed near a black hole. I hovered on the rim for a while and then it ate me up. Whoosh."

    "You dream too much. It's a sure sign of an inadequate sex life."

    "That's what you think."

"That *is* what I think."

We sat down and he dug two holes out of an orange he had brought along. He stuffed some marijuana in the top hole and lit it, sucking like mad from the bottom hole. Then he handed it to me.

"No thanks."

"You don't smoke?"

"I'm even afraid to shake my head too hard, Milo."

"Creature warmth, Clair, that's all that counts," and he drapped his long dangling right arm over my shoulder as we walked back to the Primate Center.

☆ When I first moved into the apartment, I didn't get any furniture. I didn't have any money, and the desire, after my intense domesticity with Sam, wasn't there either. I bought a secondhand TV, however, at Quality Mart, mainly for company. After an hour or two of use the thing would buzz with static and the picture would narrow to a two-inch band of squiggles. At eight in the evening, aware of my defective picture, my mother would telephone to keep me posted on all the news I had missed.

"Clair, sweetheart, did you catch that about the factory in England?"

"Nope." The weight of the world had been lifted from my shoulders at that moment by technical difficulties.

But my mother watched the news like a soap opera. Her trailer, along with the macrame, was hung with global tragedy.

"In this factory in England, Clair, they have to let the women out five minutes early so they won't get trampled. Trampled, Clair, the women won't get trampled."

I didn't say anything. What could I say? My mother, aware of the pitfalls in everything, was a stoic.

"Makes you think, doesn't it, Clair?"

"Of what, mother?" Actually, I tried hard not to think.

"Library school, law school. I'm just suggesting."

"I'm not the type, mom."

"For what? A good income, security, status, a decent wardrobe?"

I could hear the trucks passing on the freeway. The hum of traffic, in my new location, had become like the waves of the sea. I got used to it; it soothed.

"Maybe I'll become a truck driver, my own hours, high on the road, hamburgers, CB."

"Clair, being smart-ass and not thinking of your future is how you married that man, after being a straight-A student in college."

"I know." She was right, of course, and had smelled out Sam immediately.

"Very pretty," she had said of him, "but poisonous."

That was the year I had been planning to spend abroad, my junior year in the museums of Europe. Marrying Sam, I convinced myself, was the real thing, not the dry residuals. Each night, I believed, my inner eye would be in touch with the true source of art.

"You could go to night school, Clair. That's how Harry Truman made it, and he became the president. It would get you off the singles' circuit, that, at least."

"I'm not even on the singles' circuit."

"Hah, that's what you say."

Milo, over for dinner on Friday night, explained that my mother had a life-fear.

"Life-fear, baby, is like fear of death. And what she prescribes is more baby-sitting. Stave off life, stay in school, don't grow up. Grow up, Clair. Be my woman." He put his hands on my stomach. I flinched, stood up. We had been sitting on my sleeping bag on the floor, eating Wheat Thins.

For this dinner he had put his long hair in a tight Chinese braid. He wore a loose Hawaiian shirt, baggy green trousers, sandals. Milo, rail-thin and sway-back, had no bottom that I could detect.

"I'm very laid-back, myself," he said, reclining on the wall-to-wall carpet. "Listen, can Max come in?"

Max came in, smelled all the corners, settled in my empty bedroom. I served Milo canned stew on the Melmac dishes I had bought for the occasion.

"With Sam, I made stew from scratch," I explained, "bread, sourdough, and I had my own yogurt culture."

"Clair, I don't care. I understand what you're saying and where you're at and it's okay with me."

"For once, Milo, I wish you'd use your own words."

"Those are my words."

"That's what I'm afraid of."

"Don't be scared. Come here," and, putting his dish on the floor, he opened his arms.

Close-up, I could see little leaf flakes in his hair and slowly I undid his braid, combed it with my fingers.

"I used to be a male surrogate," he said.
"And?"
"I got fired. I just kept getting involved."
"You're kidding."
"Yes, I am kidding."
"King of the tree," I said.
"A man of the earth, Clair."

Initially all that silkiness, the hair, the long hair, the silky shirt, and smooth, boyish chest, intoxicated me. It seemed the best of both worlds. I hadn't been held in years—for Sam, after a while, forgot amenities. But then Milo squeezed too tightly, broke the spell. I had a sudden vision of the trees in *Snow White*. With their long limbs, they had tried to catch and keep her.

"Milo, wait. Stop, Milo."
"Huh?"
"It's no good." It also seemed sordid, clandestine.

I got up and went into the kitchen, pressed my head against the cupboards.

"God, Clair, one minute, warm and womanly, the next Miss Cold Potato. What's up? People do this kind of stuff all the time."
"I don't."
"Maybe that's the problem."
"I still feel married, Milo. I feel . . ."
"Feeling? You have feeling?"

He called Max, and they quietly left, master and dog. When I went into the bedroom later that night, I saw that Max had peed in all the corners. It was his dog's way, I supposed, of staking out territory.

☆ An old habit of mine was to read Sam's horoscope in the *Chronicle* first thing in the morning. Scorpio, proceed with caution, exciting discovery in the future, love on the horizon. Typical. Libra, straighten business affairs, clean house, avoid conflict with friends, take care of pets. Made instant coffee, went back to my sleeping bag. Saturday mornings had always been fun. What shall we do today? Sam had always asked, and we had taken picnics to the beach, gone to matinees, done something. But I had made no friends, taken up no hobbies, produced no children. Somehow being married to Sam had filled all my time. I had seen to the details, ordered his steel from U.S. Steel, scoured hardware stores for the right nuts and bolts, kept up with galleries, made the contacts. There's the man from the NEA, I nudged at parties; be charming. And Sam was a charmer. He could receive compliments like a connoisseur. Brilliantly, he got commissions, flattered the right people, tripped absently over wires, lost car keys, stumbled into afternoon affairs. Sam, Mr. Man, late for dinner again. Sheepishly, he would kick up his hooves, flash me his bashful smile. I fell again; but oh, Clair, you are my wife, just you. And why did I miss that?

March 14, 1976

Dear Sam,
Did you know that female chimps are very promiscuous. In season, they sit in a clearing, bare their bottoms to all comers.

March 15, 1976

Dear Sam,
Did you know that female chimps are very intelligent. They can learn language, wash rice, pass on culture.

March 16, 1976

Dear Sam,
Did you know that deprivation of affection makes monkeys crazy.

There had been many times when I dialed the Santa Cruz number, quickly hung up. There were many times that I saw myself going up the hill, the sleeping bag on my back. The cats would crowd around me. Sam, shy, full of remorse, would tell me solemnly that he had learned how much he loved me. I hope this new show sells, he would say, holding my hand, leaning forward in the rocking chair. If it does well, maybe we can go abroad, visit the museums of Europe. Would I like that? Oh, Clair, he would sigh, we are kin to each other. All that other stuff was just static. The true voice goes on.

I waited until ten before dialing Santa Cruz. I dialed tremulously, my throat clamping dry. One last chance, Sam, I breathed into the air. The phone rang. Then it rang and rang. I wondered where he could be. There was nothing to do in Santa Cruz after eight o'clock.

"Hello." It was a sleepy woman's voice.

"Is Sam there?"

"Samuel is busy in the studio." The voice was young, trying to sound protective. That was one thing. The second thing was that Sam never worked at night. And Sam had always been Sam, never Samuel, and the garage was the garage, not the studio. Studio?

"May I speak to Sam?" I look out across the highway to the parched hills.

"Is this the lady from the gallery?" she asked, archly.

"No, this is . . ." and I hung up very carefully, as if the phone might break.

March 20, 1976

Dear Sam,
They have learned that chimps kill their own species and just for fun. They even use tools for the job. Oh Sam, speak no evil, for . . . like King Kong. All the human traits, human straits . . .

My mother took me to lunch. The chili releno tasted like cardboard. Milo said I needed a little ecstasy for my depression. I read descriptions of dental hygiene courses, why there was a future in computer programming. Going downtown, I helped Milo select a site for his plant store, and when he asked me to go to Sausalito on the ferry with him to stay in the Sausalito Hotel, I said yes.

Riding over on the ferry from San Francisco to Sausalito, I felt nervous. Milo trilled and preened. We passed the old Alcatraz prison. I went down into the boat bar and quickly downed two gin and tonics for courage. A bit wobbly, I went topside. It was a warm night, part of the drought we had been having, and people were acting as if it was spring. Milo looked so happy I felt sorry for him. He was wearing a real suit, and I, as a matter of fact, was wearing a dress.

"Don't be scared," Milo said, as if I was going to the dentist. He gave my thigh a secret squeeze. The city lights on shore twinkled.

"They say that the Golden Gate Bridge is the end of the line for some people. They come west and can't go any further."

"Clair."

I was actually busily thinking of some ways to get out of it. A decent way. When we disembarked, I suggested we go to the No-Name Bar for a drink.

"Since when did you drink so much, Clair? If you're drunk, you won't feel a thing."

Milo took my hand and gently but firmly guided me to the hotel, which overlooked a noisy parking lot. The hotel was Victorian, with lots of lace and old wood. But the big bed swam before my eyes like a floating coffin.

"Listen, Clair," Milo said, taking off his jacket, and standing in front of me, stern as a father. "You haven't eaten; you'll get sick. I'll go out and get some sandwiches while you rest; we'll eat, and then see how you feel. It has to be two ways or no way. Understand?"

He left me there on the bed, and I could easily have ducked out, started running, never come back. He made it so easy for me that it was hard. Had he been crass or unconcerned, I could have excused myself to get some cigarettes, anything. Instead I sat frozen in my bed, waited dutifully for him to return, ate my sandwich, chewing my food twenty times on each side like a good girl, and Milo, in no rush, talked about his store, Milo's, the name spelled out in twisted ivy. I was to wear green, a good color on me, and have a watering can on the counter beside my cash register.

As he unbuttoned my dress, he said, "It's going to be fine," without specifying. "In fact, it's going to be super."

I held out my arms and he pulled the dress and then the slip over my head. He stooped down, gently unfastened my shoes.

"We suit each other, Clair," he mumbled as he kissed my neck. "Believe me."

And after a while, I did begin to believe him.

Communiqué ☆

The Laundry Room

My alarm clock buzzes a dull 7:00 A.M. The narrow band of gray cuts under the Venetian blinds, ribbons across the room. With a start, I remember that in order to go out I must wash my clothes. With my bathing suit as underwear, my nightgown as an at-home outfit, I make my way to the basement. According to the sign on the door, the laundry room opens at 8:00, but at 7:45 there is a line of us, tired, befuddled, the day stretching ahead of us like chewed-out bubble gum. Five in front of me, women I don't know, and ten washing machines, four dryers, only two blowing hot—it will be a race. At about 8:15, the super idles down the hall, swinging the keys.

"About time," the first lady says, "I have a funeral at one."

"Yeah, yeah." It is all the same to him. A dead rat planted on Christmas Day in the dryer by one of the kids in the building did not surprise him.

We ladies run for the washers, stuff like mad, retire to deck chairs. I stand up waiting and staring at my reflection in a dryer door, dream off. I remember the professor of literature who seemed to be in love with me. Me. My pinched face, Pinocchio nose, disorganized eyes. Such longing I read in his gaze, such restraint; how I wish it was then.

"Do you mind?" The lady huffily pushed in front of me. It is her clothes encased in that dryer, she will have me know.

The Unemployment Office

On my day, the A-H line always seems the longest. But the woman in front of me is glad for the wait. She compliments me on my damp and wrinkled dress, tells me I am too cute for unemployment, if I catch her gist, but this is just an opener for the story of her life. The narrative is fraught with manholes she has fallen in. Oh, child, ain't they something. I agree. The truth of the matter is that collecting unemployment is just a hobby of hers, her real vocation lying elsewhere, if I know what she means. I think I do until she opens her suitcase to show me her plans. She is rich off of interior decoration; X marks the spot. Unrolling smudgy blueprints, she explains that she has "done" Sargeant Shriver's yard, Billy Graham's yacht, Rockefeller's pantry. I tell her I was saved one night by Billy Graham in the Oakland Coliseum. When he gave the call, I swarmed down with the rest of my drunken row. A friend of mine was invited to a Peace Corps party at the Shrivers'—that is, I, too, am not without connections. Oh, a college girl, the lady says in awe. That was a long time ago, I say, thinking of another era, leafy trees. In memory it is positively antebellum, though a scant two years back. When my turn in line comes, I answer the standard questions with two yeses, one no.

1. Were you ready, willing and able to look for work during the last two weeks? yes X   no ___

2. Did you actively seek work? yes X   no ___

3. Are you receiving pension, vacation or dismissal payments? yes ___ no X

Signature: Jennifer Gardner

The Library

I stop in at the Martin Luther King, Jr., Library to see what is new. In my former life, I depended on books. Yet why, and especially now, do I feel they are worthless? Under the sign Top Ten and the Next Best are *How to Get Divorced and Feel A-O.K., How to Stay Married and Be With It, How to Build Your House out of Old Tires, How to Have Schizophrenia at Home, How to Lose a Breast and Feel 120% All-Woman, How to Give Birth in a Hot Tub,* and *How to Die Anywhere.* As I scan the titles, I feel everything is covered, no stone unturned; that is, No Reader Need Feel Uncertain anymore.

The Food Stamp Office

We in the waiting room are trying to be fairly well-dressed. We in the waiting room are trying to maintain dignity during these trying times—our life. The social workers wear jeans, strive for tackiness, try to look like people. The woman next to me tells me her life story. I only smile and she says she is a conductor and pianist trained at the University of Havana; she has led an exotic though harmless political life; she is allergic to carbohydrates. Tough on food stamps, I interject. *Mi Dios,* I can say that again, and would I help her with a biographical note for the back of the program for her next concert? Vietnamese babies cover the floor. My caseworker walks on tiptoe, as in tulips.

"Jennifer," she says.

I wish Ms. Handor would call me Miss Gardner, but I don't mention it. Ms. Handor has a tight little ass that looks great in blue jeans, shoulders that fill out her motorcycle jacket. She is almost twenty-three. I am a definite twenty-three. There is a big difference between us. I have to prove my poverty. Unemployment checks, stubs, light bills, rent. Ms. Handor notices two long-distances to New York.

"You know, Jennifer, we only count up to nine dollars on the phone bill."

I know. Those two calls saved my life. Barney's voice was like being at a concert. I sat back, let the music flow around me, wrap me, cocoon me. I love you, Jenny. And for the moment I was safe. Ms. Handor gives me a look, a look at my hair, which is very long, my final luxury. I suppose she would like me to cut it off, like the woman in the Maupassant story. And I still have blood in my veins, a small gold ring with my birthstone, which my father gave me. When I call him and my mother, I pretend I have my old job, tell them little anecdotes about the people at work—the "girls" and I went to lunch and then shopped, bridal showers, etc.

Ms. Handor has to be excused to go to the Xerox machine, which gives me a chance to study her interior decoration. She has a poster of a daisy. The petals say Today is the first day of the rest of your life.

Community Mental Health Clinic

Dr. Casey greets me in the waiting room. We have to walk down a whole length of hall together.

"Sorry I'm late," I say again. "I guess I'll just have to talk fast."

"You can begin now," he says.

Dr. Casey is a dry, seven-foot wit, a veritable basketball player of humor.

In the office he shoves the Kleenex box to me first thing. On cue I begin crying. There, there, he doesn't say. Words come hard to both of us. For me they are redundant; my story has been heard. Like those nineteenth-century unhappy Freudian ladies, I was raised in a parlor with ferns, a harp in the corner. My father hardly ever raised his voice, smoked an after-dinner cigar. My mother led the choir. And going into analysis, I was prepared for literature, mystery. Instead, we sit face to face, no dreaming off on the couch, and it is like the books in the library—upbeat, updated, full of surface cheer. With Dr. Casey as mentor, I am improving my typing and studying taxi maps of D.C. I will soon be employed, yet daily as I move from 40 w.p.m. to 50 w.p.m., from inner city to around the tourist areas, following the blue veins of the map, I feel my life seeping out from me.

As I cry, I know that if Dr. Casey were a human being, he would give me a hug, and if he were disreputable, he would do more. I mean, if anybody knows me, it is Dr. Casey. And sometimes when he thinks I am too self-absorbed to notice, I catch him looking at my legs. Of course, we leave it latent, though recently I catch myself trying to sound interesting.

The Building

My building has seen better days about fifty years ago. No pets allowed, but, on the sidewalk, dogs predominate. The rent is low, because our block is afflicted with urban blight. Yet nothing like rape or murder has ever occurred in our building. Actually, I am a block mother in my corner apartment, though I have no kids. When it rains, my charges roller-skate in the basement, play jacks and flirt by the milk machines. Once a month some of us women meet in a kind of gourmet club. Over spaghetti, we discuss modern life, the times ahead. For instance, I used to do a lot of baby-sitting on Friday nights, and now everybody stays home. However, none of us uses vibrators. We are too poor, too unsophisticated, too plain scared of shocks.

My Former Job

I worked in a special library of a social research institution dedicated to humanitarianism and to the solution of urban ills. It was a rather posh place with a fountain spurting recycled water in the lobby. In the library there were others of my background—B.A. Liberal Arts. Upstairs in the airy regions, Ph.D.'s paced the halls in turtlenecks, furrowed brows, pipes, trimmed beards. Oh yes, all very heavy stuff, but low-key; academic, but real world; theoretical, but policy-oriented. Working papers were smattered with statistics proving all beyond any reasonable doubt.

The Cafeteria at Work

This is where Barney comes in. Certain tables in the cafeteria were off-limits to the support staff, tacitly of course. And sexual pursuit was done off-grounds. However, the computer people, somewhere between support and staff, dared to have fun at their table without the researchers, what the hell did they care? They had rowdy birthday parties, what the hell did they care? Naturally, bitterness developed. Their nonchalance was so blatant, for one thing. Of course, words were exchanged. The computer people reminded the research staff that the institution depended on them for their math, the statistics in the papers, intellectual respectability in an age of science. The researchers replied that the computer people were failed scientists, degreeless technicians, dropouts.

Barney, a dropout physics student from the day he could no longer buy equipment for his dissertation experiment, said that the institution was not a think tank, as advertised, but rather a simple tank, and that useless. He added, and these are his famous last words, that the only time the research staff knew what it was doing, really knew, was when it was on the toilet.

Well.

Barney accepted an offer to become a wine salesman in New York. My boss, an M.L.S., suggested that I, too, might be happier elsewhere. Before Barney and I were good pals, but celebrating free-at-last, Barney and I became even closer; that is, he found me at close range quite interesting. The discovery was mutual.

The Bus Station

It is now Friday night, a big time at the Greyhound Bus Station. Five people are talking to themselves. One man is reading the Bible aloud, as if the bus station were Sunday school. One lady is shouting to herself, hitting herself, and jumping up and down. She focuses on a tidy young man who only wants to read his paper in peace, and she begins to harangue in a high, furious language, a spiteful, spitting language. The young man continues to read his paper avidly—any more avidly and his face would come through. Balfum, the lady says, lalala, icky. Everybody averts their eyes except me; I am staring in absolute fascination. What language, I think, what passion, the utter nerve! The Balfums, I conjecture, are a tempestuous people. They live near high waves, ruggedly. Barnacles are their national diet; holidays merit limpids.

"What are you looking at?" the lady asks me in a sudden English.

"Nothing." I am wounded.

"Jennifer?"

Barney to the rescue, and, in from New York, he looks wonderful in a vest, a flower in his lapel, wine scenting his knotty beard. Move in with him, he says first off. New York, New York, he tempts. Ah Barney, ah shucks. We run through the damp streets to my apartment. It has just rained and is still misty; the streetlights hover above us like reluctant halos. Ah Barney, how easy it would be.

My Bed, My Heart

Sometimes we go to porno flicks, to try out at home later what we have seen. Tonight, though, we stay in, lock feet, and lick French onion dip off each other's fingers. He tells me duck jokes. And they really are stories about duck life, duck problems, duck sadness and duck happiness, with lots of flap-flap, quack-quack. Then he gets serious, tells me that a foundation might fund his experiment, because he's minority. We laugh softly at this; it's all so absurd. We are sitting there without our clothes in the darkness and, when I turn on the light, yellow floods us harshly.

"As if the work itself is without merit."

"But you know it's good, Barn, you know."

"Yeah, I know."

Later when he asks me again to move up with him, I still don't have a good reason. I can't even explain it.

"I can't Barney, I just can't. I have to conquer this city."

"You like to suffer? Is that it?"

"It's not suffering."

"Let's forget it, huh?"

So we don't forget it, but he holds me as if it were all right, as if the world was working decently and the cities were the hubs of magnificent machines and we were glorious beings. Yet afterward, Barney asleep in my arms, I think of what I am giving up. I think of my room without him, the gray ribbon of morning, the stupid day. I am a fool, I say, and someday I am going to die. But that reminds me of the time I almost did die. In the waiting room of D.C. General, I thought for sure, yet within two weeks I was walking carefully down the hall in my bathrobe and slippers and down the stairs to the second floor of the hospital to use the pay phones. Strangely, the phones were right across from the rooms housing sick prisoners from the D.C. jail. They were regular hospital rooms with bars instead of doors. Usually, I received a lot of hooting and hollering, hi honey, from the prisoners. My friends on the end of the line would say Who is that? What is going on? Once, the last day I was there, I saw a new prisoner. It must have been his first day out of bed because he had to hold on to the bars for support. Pale, old, practically toothless, he watched me, and, when I was about to hang up, he said, "Listen, say hello for me, will you?"

☆ *Lessons in Love:*
A Memoir

My sex education began in 1958, Irvington, Nebraska. I was thirteen years old. My mother plunked me down on the sofa, and she, taking the rocking chair by the big, stand-up radio, gave me a quick and very nervous lecture on the facts of life. As visual aids, she used a set of melancholy diagrams from nursing school. My impression of those sketches was lasting—two nondescript, upright mammals with their skins peeled off, their sex marked by wigs, one a startling crewcut, the other a sedate June Allyson pageboy. My mother had outlined certain organs in vibrant red. Mostly muscle, she said of their composition; nerve ends, she added. Cool, blue arrows depicted glands in action. Hormones, she whispered, raising a skeptical eyebrow. All in all, I found her presentation lacking. It was too abstract, beyond my comprehension, her graphics resembling impersonal flow charts, no giggles. And her tone was somber, so full of regrets. It was terribly embarrassing. After her last word died, there was a silence in the house as the wind whipped ferociously outside. She leaned forward.

"Any questions, Zab?"

I asked her if I could now wear a bra like a certain girl in my class. My mother replied that it was a free country, but, as far as she was concerned, she wouldn't be caught dead in that French harness. Even if the president asked her to dinner. It seemed highly unlikely that President Eisenhower would invite her, an obscure, near-sighted, registered nurse from the middle of nowhere, in the dead-end of winter, up to High Society in Washington, D.C., for Beef Wellington, Shrimp Cocktail and the Works. Unlikely, but possible, which is how I was raised.

"Zab" (my nickname), "Zab, don't be afraid, take the world on, it's all yours." (I pictured the boxing ring down at the boys' gym, medals for my defeated efforts.)

"We are from pioneer stock." (She thought that said a lot.)

Although I could imagine her in a sunbonnet, hiking up her skirts to cross frontiers, ford rushing streams and all the while giving the Indian password (How?), I was less hardy. Our female relatives had come to Nebraska on the Union Pacific train; but, mail-order brides, they came to perish, new ones sent for each year at the end of winter. They died of various things:

Exhaustion

Exposure (a body could freeze on the way to the barn)

Childbirth (that was the big killer)

Smallpox (if you survived everything else)

And there was always gangrene.

Those that made it managed in sod houses, with dirt floors and no windows.

I visited a sod house with my class and felt like a mole with ribbons of soil stuffed up each nostril. But in school, we were taught a state patriotism that bordered on fanaticism. Ice cutting the land in winter, grasshoppers chewing down crops in the high, hot summer, fall and spring preludes to disaster, one simply had to love it or leave it. For instance, when the University of Nebraska football team played a home game, the whole state turned out in the school color—red.

Our house was made of gray clapboard and, standing on the edge of Irvington, seemed like the last, little block of applause before the endlessly flat fields of corn. On the side of town nearest Omaha, there was the ice-cream store where the bad kids went to flirt and smoke. Stretched between both ends was what we called the Highway, really just a wide dirt road with two deep ditches marking the sides. At home, we always entered through the kitchen door, confronted the house in stages. After the austere kitchen, the hallway—narrow, dark, and kept without a bulb to save on electricity. With no brothers and sisters, no pets to gather around me for protection, cats and dogs that would jump up and scratch out the eyes of an unwelcome intruder, I built my character fetching snacks from the kitchen at night.

"Zab, go get me some soda crackers" (gulp).

"Don't be such a scaredy-cat. The hall won't bite."

The living room was where my mother read the history of the westward expansion by the light of a lamp that had as its base a big Buddha head. Its green, droopy earlobes reached the table. I did my homework at the stamp table, with stamps from around the world and snapshots of me as a serious baby staring up from under the glass. Behind us both, the radio buzzed "A Classical Repertoire" straight from the Windy City. Outside, it was black and winter—freezing. Nightly, sitting there on my weather-locked plot of sod, I cursed both my heredity and environment. My mother, sensing adolescent anxieties, offered clumsy consolation.

"You got to go with what you have, Zab. Anyway, with lots of mammary tissue, you won't be able to run fast."

Run? Run fast? In those days a woman running brought to mind a caveman cartoon of sexual conquest, prey dragged home by a long hank of hair. I prayed for capture, dreamed of romance, and, wearing my stiff bra like twin beacons on a rocky shore, studied my mirror for signs. I was really searching for beauty, but with great foreboding saw only the traces of my pioneer stock, a smooth, round Slavic face. The only stars in my room were those painted on my ceiling—the solar system, although my mother resembled the great male lead, Spencer Tracy.

My mother. She slept on a narrow cot covered by a green blanket out on the sun porch, accompanied by a ring-red heater in winter and a twanging brown fan in summer. The one ornament in her room was a photo of my father in uniform, his cheeks painted an unnatural rosy pink. When I was very young, I thought of my father as somehow with us, woven spread-eagle into the fibers of that green army blanket. Later, I realized that a bullet had actually tunneled its way to his heart, filings to magnet, exploding his life to bits on a Pacific beach. Still later, I wondered if, as in Vietnam, they had to ship him home in a green plastic bag, the coffin sealed. For like Newton, I was a posthumous child. These facts, always with us, were never discussed. Your father died in the war, never saw you, she said one day, the air dry and hanging over us taut as an iron sheet. Facts of life, but with no diagrams. However, I remember being upstairs in my room, trying to fix a lovely dream to sleep to and hearing her downstairs praying at her bed. Oh God, she would groan.

That was my life. I grew to be sixteen. Out there on the edge of the prairies, I came to believe that structures as solid as sculpture could be made with the mind. I was an incipient mathematician, falling in love with symmetry my first day in geometry class. I was a dreamer, a shy, lonely girl. Meanwhile my mother and I kept everything going between us neat and orderly, predictable and dull—dinner in the kitchen, wash-up, homework, Saturdays for scrubbing the floor, Sundays for church. Then one night when we were sitting there in the living room, there was a knock at the kitchen door.

"Zab, go answer the door."

I glanced down the dark hall.

"Come on. I left a light on in the kitchen."

Light in the kitchen? All that wanton, wasted electricity? Perplexed, I went to the door and the man in the yard leaning back into the darkness looked like, if anybody, Superman's sidekick, Jimmy Olsen, cub reporter.

"Is Susan home?"

"Susan?" What child was he asking to come out and play in the night?

"Susan Borg Zabriski, does she live here?" He held his hat over his heart like a shield.

"Zab?"

In the space of a minute my mother had let down her tight-fisted little bun, which she wore securely fastened at the base of her neck. Her hair rippled out as if she were young.

"Horace," she trilled, "Come in. This is my daughter, Barbara Ann."

Horace Bittinger was a small, handsome man with a lined baby face. He was one of those people who start, stop, begin, a man for whom life was an awkward dancing lesson. My mother led him down the hall like a child. He plopped on the sofa, stood up, said a few words, ate them. He was dressed in a slouchy sweater, baggy pants, and his hands were like birds aflutter. His eyes, however, were luminous, and his bottom lip hung down—full, moist, ready.

"Horace is in the Stamp Club," my mother explained.

The Stamp Club, which met weekly in the library downtown, didn't hold any water with me, yet I knew that its members, like those in the Great Books Club, considered themselves the intelligentsia of Irvington.

"Horace is also the editor of the *Irvington Sentinel*."

I was not overly impressed. The newspaper specialized in lost cows, marriage announcements, high-school football scores, and who-went-to-Omaha-when. A big feature article would describe a trip to the slaughterhouse, pig crossroads of the Midwest, poor things—entering alive, leaving dead, a squeak in between. When our class went, I threw up on the bus.

"We will be working on stamps tonight, Zab," my mother said.

Big Deal. And leaving me standing there stupidly, she placed the albums on the glass-top table, my homework table. She took out her tweezers and magnifying glass from the drawer, her wax envelopes, and they dragged in two straight-backed chairs from the kitchen and set them side by side. Horace smiled sheepishly at me, his lips quivering with indecision and bravado.

"I think it's your bedtime, Zab." My mother looked at me in an entirely new way.

I didn't have a bedtime. We had been equals in the evenings, which no longer appeared boring to me; we had been companions, grownups together. Now I stomped up to my room like any angry ten-year-old and, lying in bed, looking up at my star-strewn ceiling, felt a sudden loyalty to the father I had never met. From downstairs the voices wafted up, Horace and Susan, the sounds getting softer and soft, and so, so. . . .

When I got up Sunday morning he was still there, sitting in the kitchen very matter-of-fact reading the *Omaha World-Tribune* funnies. He was also trying to smoke a pipe. The quilt was as neatly folded over the sofa back as it had been the night before. My mother lay asleep on her widow's cot.

"Good after, whoops, I mean, good morning, young lady, and what can I, I do for you?" He batted his big brown eyes, and his thin fingers went fluting up.

I didn't like him, and his flippy fingers made me nervous, but on that morning and all other Sunday mornings for almost a full year he made flapjacks for breakfast, which I loved, couldn't help it. He would toss them to the ceiling from the pan, lose them up there, catch them from behind his back. He put sliced apples in them, blueberries, even—in season—strawberries.

"Upsy-daisy, upsy-daisy," he would sing to them while I pretended not to hear. Later my mother would appear in her bathrobe and signals would start between them, of which I had no part. I'd have to flee then, upstairs, to dress for church. Furiously I would stuff my bra, fiddle with my straight, stringy hair and press to bruising my passion-pink lipstick. I would fume at my juvenile dress, which inevitably tied in the back. Meanwhile, my mother would pull up her hair, become her regular self.

We were Catholics, bad Catholics, terrible Catholics, but Catholics nonetheless. I was taught by my priest that God loved me, that His love was infinite and pure. Like all love, also, I learned later, it was irrational and costly. I liked church. Sermons I never listened to, but I was curiously moved by the rhythm of the mass. Parts would catch me unaware, such as when Father said, "Come, let us celebrate the mystery of our faith."

Horace was not a Catholic, so we would have to leave him behind on the steps of the house, waving us good-by. Down the road, I would look back every few minutes, checking. First he was the awkward boy-man, then, diminishing as we went up the road, he would be a wooden puppet, dwindling to a stick figure, collapsing to a bird with slapping wings, a napkin magically out on its own, finally a dot, a nothing.

My mother couldn't take Communion on Sunday after Horace's visits and went to Communion during the week following Confession. That same summer, 1961, Kennedy's first summer in office and when the country seemed reborn, I, too, began having trouble fitting in Communion and Confession.

I met Brice at the ice-cream store where we both worked. He had been in my trig. class, a tall, serious boy with glasses and longish, soft hair—wild wheat. During ice-cream lulls, we smoked and chatted in the back room and very shortly, with few preliminaries (we were both self-declared iconoclasts), began making love under my whirling solar system while my mother worked the late shift at the hospital. Once a month we drove in his father's old pick-up truck to Omaha, where they didn't know us, to buy Trojans. Terribly proud of ourselves, we saved the little sacs, which when filled dropped down like the Buddha ears, all the wisdom of the East. With ceremony, we buried them in even rows out in the backyard under my mother's clothesline, popsicle sticks marking the spots. The nights she was home, those hot, still Nebraska summer nights, I stood at my upstairs windows dreaming down at them, conjuring a sprouted army. My kindergarten.

We were two shy people who had found each other. It was an intensely private thing, full of idiosyncrasy and wonder. I came to know every filling in Brice's teeth, the bumps of the vertebrae down his skinny back, the pink folds of his small ears. I was touched by the sight of his Adam's apple, his voice on the phone gave me reason for living, and seeing him at work every day made dying possible. That summer I accepted my flat chest, my saucer-plate face, even my hair, but I expected my final flowering of both mind and body to take place out of state, at college, in the wonderful world at large. Brice was to go to MIT, and I hoped for Radcliffe. We plotted life off-campus in a dinky apartment, together, avant-garde bohemians. The real Bohemians, the inarticulate country people of our youth, we wrote off entirely, for we planned to never return to Nebraska, home of the Cornhuskers.

In the fall, the night before we took the college boards, we drove to a horror movie to get our minds at ease. It was already freezing by then and we slipped and skidded along the highway there and back. Twice I had to get out of the car to check for scratches. After the movie we sat in our car for an hour, the engine running for heat.

"I want to suck your blood," Brice kept repeating like Dracula as he placed big, red welts up and down my neck (monkey bites, we called them).

Wearing a scarf and boasting a fever of 103°, I flunked the next morning. In due time, the rejection letter came, but Brice, healthy as a hog, immodestly won a National Merit. Our pact of whither-thou-goest collapsed under the weight of his unilateral success. Our garden of delights also sank. Snow covered the land, and I felt myself buried within a loneliness that muffled all hope.

My mother suspected, I suppose, but she didn't ask. She still had Horace and Saturday nights. She worked at the hospital and I graduated, again went to work in the ice-cream store. At night I counted the stars on my ceiling, those cold, indifferent, faraway stars. By July, I began to remember that those tiny points of light had been painted by my mother's warm hand. Putting on overalls, consulting a map of the heavens, climbing the ladder, she had delicately brushed them on, small strokes, everything to scale. I told myself those stars were dead. Yet, their light still beamed forth. And our sun was alive, not cold, holding us to our charted course. My mother had wanted me to look at those stars, to dream, to aspire. I began to discover points of gravity, to recuperate. The University of Nebraska no longer seemed like the end of the world.

That summer on Wednesday nights, I used to help Horace get his paper out. I did the layout for the society page, which meant marriage announcements outlined in a narrow black tape. One night, standing down the row from Horace at the high, slanting table, under the bright lights, I came upon the following announcement:

> Mr. and Mrs. Boniface of Irvington are proud to announce the engagement of their daughter, Miss Debbie Boniface, a recent graduate of Lincoln High, to Mr. Horace Bittinger, Editor-in-Chief of the *Irvington Sentinel*.

I looked down the row. Horace seemed very busy.

> The couple plan a September wedding, followed by a honeymoon in Chicago. They will reside in Omaha, where the bride will be employed as a claims adjustor with Mutual of Omaha and the groom will be a city news reporter with the *Omaha World-Tribune*.

Reading that news, I recalled the theme to a radio program I always listened to on Sunday night. It was "The Whistler," "The Shadow," or maybe "The Fat Man." Following some scary music, the words went: "Who knows what evil lurks in the heart of men?"

"You get around, Horace," I said.

He stiffened, shrugged, reached for his pipe, changed his mind, grinned idiotically, looked as if he might cry. My mother had helped him gain self-confidence, but the old, unsure mannerisms returned at times.

"How old are you, Horace?"

I knew he wasn't any recent high-school graduate. I put him at about twenty-eight.

"Thirty-four, Zab," he admitted apologetically. "I want to start my family."

My mother was a good thirty-six and, to me, old. I could not imagine her "starting a family." I was her family, soon to start college. I looked at the photo of the engaged couple. She wore a sweater set, a pointy bra like mine, a string of pearls, and the June Allyson hairdo of my mother's drawing of female for my first lesson in love.

"Will this be new? New news to my mother?"

He nodded. I groaned. She read Horace's crummy rag like Gospel. And she, more than I, was a very private person.

First, she cut her hair. Back to Spencer Tracy or the old Gertrude

Stein. After work, she sat on the sofa, the stamp album inert on her lap, the green Buddha lamp off, the radio buzzing between stations. She got careless with herself—she who had been so fastidious with her appearance, dressing in the morning under the tent of her nightgown, now roamed the house with her bathrobe open. I saw that, though she still did not wear a bra, she did hold up her stockings with an unbending, thigh-length girdle.

For days we hardly said a word to each other. Hello, good-by, see-you-later. I brooded about her while I packed the ice cream, smoked silently by myself, and tried to work out a calculus problem in a vain attempt to understand the concept of a limit. I thought of what I could say to her in that lonely house, which at night seemed like a big train snaking west across the prairies. I wondered what comfort I could offer as we sat across from each other with two white plates in front of us, napkins folded, silverware at attention, glasses turned down against any free-floating germ. We were stranded there, marooned on a green oilcloth in a checkerboard sea of linoleum where once flying flapjacks had cavorted. We were so . . .

"Mom," I said one night close to college.

"Mmmm?" She studied her plate for specks.

"Mom," I repeated, taking her hand, holding it to my cheek.

"Ah, Zab," and she began to cry very softly, delicately.

"It's okay, Mom."

"No, it isn't. It will be okay, but not now."

A late summer wind, hot without mercy, tore around the house.

"When you get older, Zab, wounds take longer to heal."

I didn't say anything.

"It will heal," she said slowly. "It will heal, but right now, right this very minute, it hurts so much. You know, Zab, so much."

"I know," I said. "I know."

Me at the Gas Station

My mother names me Flynn after the movies, but from small my friends call me Patchy, and that is the name that stick. As a boy in Port-of-Spain, Trinidad, I specialize in mending and making. Out of scrap alone I do henhouse, pigeon coop, table, chair, anything that take hammer, nail, glue. But the funny thing is that with all my talents I was not able to keep my own marriage in one piece. Whistler say that it not my fault. He tell me it is the times—sixties. He tell me it is America—Brooklyn, New York, to be exact. And he tell me it is Lotus Lee—a woman gone crazy with American glamour. Me, I am not sure about the sixties and Lotus, but let me tell you one thing, the winter in America had to be the worst of my life. That was when I work for Whistler at the gas station.

The way Whistler acquired his gas station is by coming from Trinidad to the States on student visa. According to Immigration, the man come to study television repair at Westinghouse Tech. He register for class, that true enough, but, from the minute he up, he studying the taxi map of the city for hacker's license, and from there he cruising night and day hacking, hacking, hacking. Meantime his wife, some country girl from the bush, taking in twenty little kids to baby-sit in the apartment like it school for babies, and Whistler, he pick them up in his cab like it bus and he bring them home at night, and pretty soon the wife in a big house and he, Whistler, standing up in front of his Amoco station, hands in his Amoco pants pockets watching the action on Florida Avenue. That's America for you.

But though the man get rich, he keep his heart soft. What I mean is that he hire problems. The time I working for him we have a Persian at the pumps. He came up to the States as student and know plenty of maths, but mainly he specialize in the Shah and is in constant danger, he explain, from the SAVAK. We all play cards together in the back room after work, where Whistler keep a pot of curry goat going on the hot plate. The other mechanic is Moxie from Israel. His troubles he keep private but, for one, we know his wife die and that he learn mechanics of tanks. He tell us that in Israel the people drive crazy-fast due to nerves. Whistler say he can imagine. All of Moxie's jokes are sad, yet the man have a good spirit. He put up a sign in Hebrew under the Amoco. It say Patchy, Moxie, Mohammed and Whistler's Garage. Whistler's sign say Foreign and American Mechanics on Duty. Half-true.

In the back of the station is a big field with junk and weeds, certain plants, I understand, that belong to Mrs. Olga, my landlady, and she also a Indian Spiritual Reader, and beside the field is a Roy Rogers restaurant. Across the street is the row house where I live, where Lotus and I lived together for a month. Upstairs is the apartment and downstairs is Mrs. Olga. After my wife leave, I spend more time at the station and sometimes I visit Mrs. Olga. Sometimes I watch "Sesame Street" on the TV. It is company.

The difficulty started, I believe, because Lotus Lee came up to the States first. She come up with a friend who was going to hairdressing school and Lotus, herself, apply for Washington School for Secretaries. Since I do not have a secondary-school certificate, I cannot apply for student visa and have to wait for ninety-day visitor's visa. At the beginning she send me letters, but then they stop. When finally I get my visa and step off the plane, I am surprised to see that my wife have her hair piled up high on her like she trying to be her own tall building. At night she wind a roll of toilet paper around her hair to get what she call her beehive stiff. She is a receptionist, she say, and have a big desk, a big telephone, and a big pad for messages. Besides the toilet paper, she cover her face with white, bleaching cream.

"Lotus Lee, why you put on so much grease? I don't want to kiss grease."

"I need to look young, Patch. Everyday I must meet the public."

"You are twenty-three. Do you want to look ten?" With her hair up, I think she look thirty, but I do not say it. Instead I unpack my sweetbread, some cake her mother sent up, pepper sauce and a ripe mango.

"Did anybody see you with all that food, Patch?"

"No."

"Thank God. This is not a kitchen country, you know, and me, I am through with kitchen life, simple people."

"Simple people is who love you, girl, and that kitchen you bad-mouthing pay you way up to Glamourland, yes?"

At home we lived with my family, which she never like. But they had room, what is the fuss? My people run a little cook shop and my father do the main cooking. If he see pot, he got to cook just like I see stick, I got to carve. On Sundays my father play dominoes under the tree in the backyard. Yes, they are simple. People happy and they don't look for reason. On Mondays my father make stew chicken. Tuesday is crab and callaloo and Wednesday be pilau. There be five tables in the front room and clean oilcloth on the tables. The people who eat are country people who work in the city and cannot get home for lunch, and the night people are the widowers who have nobody to cook for them. After all the customers eat, the family sit down together and eat what would spoil the next day. My big sisters come with plates to fill up for their families and we always give some to Whistler's mother next-door. She is a seamstress who raise up Whistler by herself. Near Carnival time you see her light bulb swinging bright on its cord late into the night and the sequin cloth spill through her hand like a silver net cast into the river to catch the Hindu moon.

Lotus and me, we be cousins. We are both Chinese with some African, but Lotus look all Chinese and me, well, when I start looking for a job in America and must put race, I have to ask Lotus what to put.

"You are one black nigger, Patchy Wong," she tell me not so nice.

Still, I think, finding a job in America be easy, but I see soon that with no green card, no official training, no union, I am in trouble. Everywhere I go they want me to fill out form, which I am not too good at. Which is why when I find Whistler, I know God is good. With Whistler there be no questions, no put your X or any such nonsense. He feel same way and does not like to be told anything. Immediately Lotus and I move across the street so I can be near my work. I think everything will be fine. But that's when it all start.

I up a month when somebody from Lotus's work give a party. She tell me that she who is in "public relations" must keep up "relations" and that as a married woman how would it look if she go to party without her husband. Now, I am sure that she had been to party without me when I back in Trinidad, but I reply that I will go if Whistler and his wife go too. She say back that Trinidadians have to drag along the whole island wherever they go. In America, she say, people can stand alone without friends. Suddenly she the expert on Civilization. That's the trouble with America, I say back. They don't have friends.

But we go, and in my heart I know it will be fatal. The month is October, I up a month and already the place look like the land of the dead. It is cold, the sky a heavy gray and the trees reach up without a leaf to their branches. I forget to mention that we in costume. Not even Carnival and on a regular day, I dressed like a cowboy. Whistler go in his old red devil suit and his wife in a long dress, and Lotus, let me tell you, was practically in a bathing suit. In the back of Whistler's cab, I tell her that a West Indian woman is sure of herself after she is married and don't have to show her parts if she know what I mean. She tell me she is not a "West Indian woman."

"We married, girl, it settled. What more can a woman want?"

She tell me in a hiss that we have to talk about our relationship. Seriously.

"Relationship seriously. What is that?"

"We outgrow each other, Patch."

Whistler and his wife in front pretend they not hearing, but every once in a while Whistler look up at his mirror. I see, he sees, he understands.

"Outgrow," Lotus repeats.

"Me, I was grown up when I marry you, and too old for cat and mouse, boy-girl nonsense. Stop playing with your life, Lotus."

"We need to talk."

"You will talk yourself right out of business, girl."

"Our marriage . . ."

But we are there and, down in the basement around the bar with the fake, plastic plants, I see I am going to have to be dead-drunk to stay one minute. First thing I notice is that it is all black. Now we are black, too, but Americans, they be different. They shake your hand, call you brother, and then they forget your name. While Whistler and me at the bar, one of them comes up to me in his cowboy suit.

"I understand you boys are from the islands," he began, badly.

"Yes," Whistler answer, not giving any life story.

"*Habla espanol?*"

"King's English," Whistler answer, and it seem enough, for the man leave us in peace.

"Who was that masked asshole?" Whistler ask, and we laugh, drink some more scotch, look around at the imitation fun. I notice Miss Lotus Lee Wong is arranged on the couch. But pretty soon the liquor doing its job so I ain't worry about her and when the Lone Ranger makes his way over again, I see him like a wavy mirage bubbling across some long desert in a Wild West movie.

"What do you do?"

Now in America that is big question.

"I study television repair at Westinghouse Tech," Whistler answer, because you can never tell who the Immigration man checking up.

"They have TV in the islands?"

"And they all be in color," Whistler tell him. Which remind me of how a lady down the street from us make her TV into color. She just put up her Christmas cellophane paper over the screen.

Just about then somebody put on a Harry Belafonte record. "Island in the Sun." It make me sick how the man come down and make millions off our music, but I smile. The cowboy smile back showing me his full set of teeth. I don't know how it happen, but I just feel to splash my drink in his teeth just like I once saw in a movie and that is exactly what I did. It was so amazing that even I did not believe it, but the next thing Whistler pushing me up the stairs, and out through the house, the women following behind. Outside it so cold, my breath caught in my throat, but I had to pee so bad, I have to open up in the gutter and, with the hot water cracking the flecks of ice, all my anger drain out. Except that Lotus be there and she is just about crazy with disgust. When we got home, she ask for divorce.

"Divorce," I say. "Are you out of your mind? Poor people don't get divorce."

"What they do? Jump out the window?"

That night she move out to her friend, the hairdresser, with just a few things.

"Go," I say to myself in the darkness. "Go on. You'll be back."

☆ That winter Whistler put a heater in the back room where we play poker. He tell us that some Koreans want to buy the station. He is considering it. Winter is cold. Moxie looks scared at the thought of the Koreans. And Mohammed tell us it is CIA in disguise. He imagine them out there in the big frozen field hiding in the weeds waiting to close in. But Mrs. Olga, my landlady and the Indian Spiritual Reader, went out one night and cut down all the weeds, bringing them in to dry in her basement. I was surprised when I looked out of my window and saw her cutting them down in the moonlight. And then when I was in the basement washing my clothes I was surprised to see them hanging up by the water pipes.

"Is it true," I ask Moxie during our poker game, "that the Jews can speak to God directly?"

"I pass," Moxie answer.

I have a full house in my hand, the best hand I ever had, and I am wondering what Whistler is holding. Mohammed is wearing the mask he make for demonstrations against the Shah. I say it is not fair to wear a mask for poker, plus it remind me of that masked stranger at the party that ended my marriage.

Whistler say, "Oh, let him wear his damned mask if he wants."

"And Moxie always look the same, win or lose," I add.

Whistler chew the end of his mustache, give me the evil eye.

"Is it true that the Hebrews don't believe in heaven and hell?"

"Patch," Whistler warn.

"Just wondering."

"It's all right," Moxie say, giving me his sad smile.

"It is this, Mox. If you don't have heaven, what is the point?"

"Patch." Whistler is doing his growl.

"The here and the now," Moxie answer.

"But are you having fun, Mox?"

"Fun is not the point."

"What is the point?"

"Patch, you tell us the point."

"Lotus is gone three months, and I am miserable."

"We know, Patch, and stop wetting the cards. Forget that horse. I tell you the girl no good from a long time."

"But I am a lover, Whistler."

"He is a lover," Mohammed agree through his mask.

"The real thing," Moxie add, shrugging his shoulders.

"Patch is an idiot," Whistler say.

I win the pot, take my turn at the pumps, then go in for the next game.

"Is that Reader downstairs doing you any good?" Mohammed ask.

I shrug. I go every week for a reading. Mrs. Olga say it takes time.

"If you go home, I take you to obeah man in Saint James for your *tabanka* over Lotus Lee," Whistler say.

"What is obeah?" Moxie wonder.

"Magic. Some believe," Whistler say, "that the obeah men from the first slaves that run off into the hills. They do miracles, and the one in Saint James the best. There was a boy, a young boy who ain't talk for three months, not one word. His mother get worried, so she took him up on the hill to the obeah man. He had the boy sit down in a chair and he walk all around him looking, looking. Then he pry open the boy's mouth and look deep inside, checking out the teeth and the tongue. He walk around the chair again, thinking, thinking. Then he go into the next room where he keep his supplies and pick out a dead, fresh-plucked chicken and very tippytoe he creep back into the room and behind the boy so the boy ain't see him. Very quiet, the obeah man swing the dead chicken behind his back by the legs and wap, he come down hard with the chicken on the boy's back."

"What the boy do?" I ask Whistler.

"The boy let out one big scream. 'Oh Gawd, Oh Gawd, man, stop hitting me with that dead chicken.' But the obeah man ain't stop. No sir. He swing the chicken around and around, coming down, wap, right on the boy's back. 'Oh, obeah man, leave me be,' the boy cry out, and he take off, running down the hill crying for mercy. 'That be two shillings, please,' the obeah man tell the mother."

"It was a shock," I say. "That is all."

"Well, it work, don't it?"

I go home broke, notice that Mrs. Olga is up. Sometimes she makes a tea for me to calm my nerves. The first time I came, she answered the door in a scarf, fuzzy slippers and a long, loose dress. Her skin look like a wallet and, under scarf, the hair is thin. But she is not old, for two children hold her skirt like she is mommy.

"Ten dollars for the complete reading," she tell me that time.

I notice the sign on her window, which have Indian man with feathers that it say Reading, $5.00. She reply that the sign is five years old and the price go up a dollar a year.

"Okay, complete reading."

I follow her through the apartment to a room I never seen before.

The two little kids trail behind us. In the room behind a curtain of gold beads is just a table, two chairs from the kitchen, many-size candles lit and blazing mirrors, pictures of the Holy Mother and a diploma on the wall. It say Certified and Ordained, The Reverend Mrs. Olga Mislash, 1965, Culver City, California.

"Go play," she tell the children as we settle down in the chairs and she ask me to open my left hand. She bounces her middle finger off my palm and then ask for the other hand. She looks at them hard and long, and sighs.

"Thursday your lucky day, five your lucky number."

"Which line say five my lucky number?"

"That is a professional secret."

"Thirteen my lucky number."

She doesn't smile.

"In truth, Mrs. Olga. Listen, I up in the States two weeks and this lady come by the station selling the number, and I play thirteen twice. Then next week she bring me $500, and with that I bought my dinette set, which my wife has now stole from me."

"Lucky? A stolen dinette set? Anyway, I am not talking about the past. It is the future I deal with. From now on your lucky number is five, and I can see that you are a man who needs to understand his luck. You are a good man, Mr. Wong, a good husband, but people take advantage of your good nature."

At that I have to sit back. She was right, completely ten-dollars right.

"If you want me to pray for you, make novena," she clears her throat, "that will be ten dollars more."

"You mean I don't have good luck coming to me?"

"I am suggesting better luck."

I can smell something cooking in the back of the apartment. It is sweet and spicy at the same time, maybe cinnamon soup, and I recognize that it is the smell that I always smell in the house, only stronger.

"My wife coming back soon?"

The lady put her two fingers over her eyes again, press hard. I lean forward, the candles sputter up and even the Virgin seems to stretch toward me out of her picture like she listening in, too. All of a sudden I feel something tweak my bottom.

"Oh, Gawd," I shout.

"Hugoito," the lady screams, "leave Mr. Wong alone. Mommy is working."

Everything get quiet again. She press her eyes; I hold my breath.

"You should not dwell in the past and hope to repeat what is gone. You must come to understand yourself and forget your wife. It will take work, Mr. Wong, and time, but together we can . . ."

"Olga, Olga, I'm home."

"Hugo, is that you?" She leap up, pushes open the curtain. "Excuse me, my husband is home," she say over her shoulder and it is a mad rush to the door. I slip out, go back to the station.

Mohammed, over a ranch burger at Roy Rogers, tells me that Mrs. Olga is not even from Paraquay. Maybe from California, and her husband, Hugo, is Hungarian refugee who fix watches at Korvette's. He tell me, also, that Roy Rogers stuff his horse, Trigger, when he die and keep him. Very interesting, I say, not at all interested. I tell him my one experience with cowboys. Big gun in the West, Mohammed say. Mohammed reads a lot. I tell him the last thing I ever read was *A Tale of Two Cities* in school, and that was too much for me. That night three medical students from the hospital join our poker game. It is Big Money in the game and Whistler is nervous, Moxie very quiet, and Mohammed sit out sewing his mask. I look around, on the shelf are boxes of spark plugs, tires, pumps, hoses, starters, a little map of Trinidad and photo of Whistler's wife and two kids in front of the new house. She is a nice lady, but thick, definitely somebody's mother. There plenty like that in Trinidad, with the apron around their waist. Hanging on the wall behind the shelf is a picture left over from the last owner. It is mostly the American flag coming out of a fluffy cloud over a barn and a church and underneath the church written in fancy letters, it say:

> People raised in a free country—nourished mentally by free schools and a free press, gainfully employed in a free enterprise and strengthened morally by the free religion of their own choice— are better able to develop. Let us be alert to any foreign ideology which would undermine and deprive us of our greatest possession—The American Way.

The last words—The American Way—is done in gold letters. I ask Whistler once what foreign ideology mean and he tell me it is soccer. That night when I go home, I discover that the bed is gone. Everyday something goes, bit by bit. I am at work, come home, and the couch gone. I be out buying food and the lamp whisk away. Behind my back, the chair march down the stairs. The dinette set went in fifteen minutes while I down in the basement washing my clothes under all the drying plants. My bureau went while I was shaving, clothes dumped on the floor. Of course, the TV the first to go. That leave right after Christmas. But the bed, that the worst. I had kept Whistler posted of the details, letting him know, day by day, but when the bed go I don't even feel to go to work. I make my clothes in a pile and lie down with them, watching the ceiling. Morning comes and goes. I can hear cars on the road, the little kids playing downstairs. The sun hit my feet, travel to the window, disappear, and, as it starts to get dark, I hear footsteps and the door open.

"She took the bed," I explain to Whistler, not looking at him.

"I can see that, Patch. I told you to change your locks long time, teach that horse a good lesson. Your name should be Pillow, not Patch, the way she abuse you."

"It's not the furniture, Whistler."

"You better get up off that floor, man."

"I studying the rabbit on the ceiling, Whistler, and sometime I see her face."

"You better get up off that floor, Flynn Wong, or you be studying the inside of a monkey house. That woman take bad advantage over you, but you no need to get a *tabanka* over it."

He pull me up and lean me against the wall.

"You eat anything lately?"

"Not hungry."

"What nonsense you talking. The woman ain't steal your belly, did she?"

So, Whistler take me down to Rita's for a nice roti wrapped around some chicken curry. Nice break from ranch burgers.

"You know, Patch," Whistler tell me. "You lucky this happen to you in Brooklyn. Did you know that there be more women to man in this city? They be desperate, man, and no time you find a new, better one, somebody who will cook your food and keep your house, and grateful for the opportunity."

We go back to the station. Moxie and Mohammed say they worried about me. We settle in for a nice quiet game. Spring is coming soon, they tell me, it will make big difference. At about nine I do my turn at the pumps, come back in. Moxie is winning for a change. Mohammed is reading aloud to us out of *The Book of Records*. He is just at the part about the fattest man in the world buried in a piano case when we hear sirens, and the door burst open and three big police tell us, "Up against the wall, fingers spread."

"The SAVAK," Mohammed cries out like he wounded already.

"The Immigration," Whistler hissed through his teeth.

"Vice Squad, Drug Detail, as if you didn't know," the police say. They tell us to drop our pants and they check all along our sides and inside, too. They make us open our mouths wide and feel around our teeth. And then with us standing there, our pants around our heels, they pull out the boxes on the shelves and open the drawers tipping them over, and with long knives they slash tires, poke in corners. They break open a camera, and rip out the film. We have ladies' supplies just in case, and they pull out the cotton. All the time I don't know what they want, and I can smell something burning.

"Something is burning," I say.

"Shh," Whistler whisper.

"You better believe something is burning. Where is Olga Mislash?"

Whistler signal me a signal. I say nothing.

"Mislash. We're looking for Mislash."

The smell of burning gets stronger, and out of the corner window I can see flames from the field. It is the cinnamon soup smell.

"The Palm Reader Indian?"

Mohammed knocks me with his elbow and Moxie arch his eyebrows up like he used to trouble.

"Mislash?" The man shake me a bit. I shrug.

"I bet," the police say.

So they take us in the wagon downtown, the siren roaring. When we get there, Mohammed, who know about arrests, calls his lawyer, who arrive in about two minutes like he live next-door. He asks to see the search warrant and, when they show him, he tell them right off that they busted in the wrong address. He tell them they liable for suit. The lawyer drives us back to the station and we go into the Roy Rogers, which is open all night, for some milk shakes, Whistler's treat. From the window we can see little flames licking the edges of the field.

"What is it?" I ask.

"A real cash crop," the lawyer tells us.

I still do not understand, and after a while I see the police arrive at the house, and Mrs. Olga, her husband and two children are bundled out and put in the wagon for the trip downtown.

"I don't understand," I say again, "but I know one thing . . ."
Moxie smiles.
"Soon as it gets light, Whistler, I'm packing."
"Ah, Patchy," Moxie say.
"Me too," Whistler answer. "I'm going to sell out to the Koreans. Let them have it."
"Maybe I can sell a rug," Mohammed says, "and buy the station."
"Maybe you can."
"It would be nice, Mo, if you could," Moxie brightens up.

The lawyer looks interested, too. And when the sky begins to go from black to light gray, I go across the field scorched to the ground, parts smoldering. It is like a scene from Hell. I climb the stairs in the empty house, take down my suitcase, pile in the clothes. Lucky for me, I have no furniture and my ticket is round-trip.

History ☆

When I think of our brief marriage twenty-six years ago, before freedom rides and busing, it is like recalling pages out of a history book. In photographs Marcus, with his scalp-short hair, the part properly shaved, his shoes shined to a mirrory sheen, looks like a member of the Southern Christian Leadership Conference. I, with my open, white-girl smile, long bundle of blond hair, and dirty toes in California sandles, am a caricature hippie.

In 1960 all the newspapers in the nation's capital listed housing under White or Colored. Wherever I called, the landlords' first question always was: White? Both, I'd answer. We are both. Immediately, on the other end, there would be a sudden intake of breath as if I were a crank call or obscene or had let loose a big, bad snake into the wire which was inching forward, making its way up the wire to bite off an ear, pinch a nerve. They would let down the phone that carefully.

"My husband is white," Mrs. Trakled had explained over the phone, and she brought it up again when she was showing us the upstairs apartment she had available. She and the Reverend lived downstairs. It was an immaculate rowhouse in a nice Negro neighborhood with clipped lawns, rosebushes, and green and white awnings unfurled over freshly painted porches.

"The thing is," Mrs. Trakled said, "is that I am picky about my tenants." She looked at Marcus approvingly. "I understand you are studying to be a doctor at Howard University. My, my, a medical man." Marcus had worn a three-piece suit for our interview, carried an umbrella and looked quite the Englishman—from the colonies. Mrs. Trakled was in purple. It was a plum dress for the Grand Tour, with pleated handkerchiefs springing clusters of violets pinned to her shoulders. She look like Mercury on errand, wings at ready-alert. "And you, my dear," she said turning her motherly gaze on me, "working for the *Post*? I'm a professional woman, too."

Mrs. Trakled's sign hung in the front yard:

The Reverend Mrs. Trakled
Lessons in the Piano for Young Ladies

"Actually," she continued, "my husband is white-white. A man of the cloth."

I imagined ghost. Marcus gave me a look like Klu Klux Klan, but rabbit was more like it. The Reverend, who mysteriously materialized when we signed the lease across the grand piano, was albino and just about as old as Methuselah, with blinking, pink eyes and an embarrassed, bashful smile.

"The Reverend, once one of God's chosen orators, is now a man of few words," Mrs. Trakled explained. "We are from Mississippi, you see, and, would you believe it, we couldn't get married down there, had to ride separate cars up to D.C. and here we are."

"It sounds like the Underground Railway," I said.

"What say?" The Reverend shuffled forth, leaning in toward me.

"They are newlyweds, Rev.," Mrs. Trakled giggled.

☆ "Underground Railway, really Joanna." We were packing like mad to make the move to the Trakleds'. I could hardly wait.

"Can I help it that I was a history major?"

"Yes indeedy."

"Can you hug me, Marcus, in Virginia, where you come from?"

"Are you crazy?"

I was. It gave me leeway. But Marcus was Mr. Rational. In Control. It took me five minutes to stuff my meager belongings in my straw suitcase. We were staying at his ex-roommate's. Marcus folded all of his stuff neatly, arranging it in piles before putting it in his trunk. I noticed the letter from his mother. Back in Virginia, half a step out of Washington, she did not approve of me. Her letter had left enough space between the lines for me to evoke the whole scene, one Marcus had once described—the rickety front porch of the P.O. boasting a bevy of overalled, tobacco-chewing Guardians of Justice. On the side of her house hung an iron washtub, and under the one tree in the yard was an old carseat with a spring sticking out like a corkscrew. Marcus said his mother made him wear a clothespin on his nose every Saturday and that he was scrubbed Saturday night hard enough to bleed (read bleach). Yet she didn't like me, I, who was a natural.

My mother, at home in California amid her cats and dusty pottery, dashed off a quick note (more later) stating that she knew I would always marry somebody interesting. What she had in mind, I knew, was somebody larger than life—a Paul Robeson–John Henry type, a Byron or a Browning. Somebody dark and dangerous, and definitely *très beau*.

Marcus and I had met at Howard University, E. Franklin Frazier's course, "Negro in the United States." It was a history course and I felt pretty historic myself, for I was the only white person in the class and, from what I could see, on campus, save one exchange student from Oberlin who assiduously avoided me.

"How do you like Howard?" Marcus and I were upstairs in the library, late spring, fans already set up on the long, lacquered tables. Outside the open windows, the air was still and dense even though it was eight o'clock at night.

"Fine," I answered, moving my long hair out of my eyes, giving the man a good look. He wore wire-frame glasses. Nobody did then, and he had an old-fashioned, professorial look about him.

"Be honest." His wrists were thinner than mine and his fingers were long. You could play the harp in heaven, I thought.

"I'm always honest," I lied. Downstairs in the lobby there was a portrait of General Howard, blue eyes, no left arm. The old Union general had gone from freeing slaves to killing Indians. The first students at Howard were not freemen, but Chinese. It was a place full of contradictions. Yet, familiar.

"It's like a white school," I said. Every afternoon, light-skinned sorority girls linked arms and sang on the quad. It was like *my* college.

"So we're disappointed, are we?" He had a condescending, slightly humorous way of looking at me over the top of his glasses. He made me feel amusing.

"Surprised," I said.

"We," and he gently put one of his long, brown fingers on my wrist as if feeling for the pulse, "are human just like everybody else. Not morally superior, particularly wise. Just people. Suffering is not a good teacher, all publicity to the contrary."

I should have listened to those words, for they would have provided a key to the language of our marriage. Instead, at that time, I didn't see how prim he was and only noted how different he was from my counterparts at the bookstore were I worked, those pale and pasty male versions of myself. Marcus was older, a hundred times more interesting and, of course, mysterious as Egypt. My heart did a fast flutter-butter, and I knew I was done for. Once before I had been in love, during college, and that had been pure disaster. He was Oriental.

"I'm going to New York next week." Strains of the A.K.A. song wafted up. A sorority sister was passing by. The fans moved left and right on their stiff necks like sunflowers following the sun. I knew it was presumptuous to tell him I was going away, that is, as if he were interested, but I took the risk.

"I'll visit you," he answered. "I mean it." And we exchanged names and addresses. His handwriting was small, elegant, a stylized code.

"Joanna Kandel," he read. "And where is this in New York?"

"The Village."

"Ah, of course."

"No, really, it's just a cheap sublet, I can't let the opportunity . . ."

"Of course not."

"Are you laughing at me again?"

"Good gracious no." He raised his hands in surrender. "Why would I do that?"

☆   The job I found in New York was worse than the one I left in Washington. Not a bookstore, which is all a B.A. in History from Mills College netted me in Washington, but at a Discount China store. I would say discounted discount china and narrow as a ship's galley with place settings, each one an extraordinary bargain, rising to the ceiling like the Leaning Tower of Pisa. A stroll to the back of the store provided seasickness, and the bathroom was always at high tide.

"*Qué pasa?*" Some cute Puerto Rican guys worked as packers in the storeroom. I had to go by them all on the way to the bathroom.

"Degeneration of values in the western world, *hombres*," I'd answer, picking out a handy strip of Japanese newspaper from the packing crate. I read: " 'Likewise the eastern world.' Nobody committing hari-kari anymore, what *is* this world coming to, yen for life reported on all fronts."

They'd stare at my hairy legs and armpits as if they had never seen such before and give me the old thumbs-up. Yes, we understood each other. Ditto the other salesperson, with whom I had a deep rapport. She was an Argentinian, refugee from the Peronistas, and had hopes of meeting a dentist in America, moving to Queens. I told her a little about Marcus. Not all, of course.

Friday nights and the city st⋯ ⋯king a good 92°, I would do the rounds of the air-conditioned ⋯ ⋯ew and far between in 1960. I especially like the ones wi⋯ ⋯riums, green bubbling, sea divers, startled sea horses. But r⋯ ⋯r would I get comfy on my stool than some lech would hur⋯ ⋯ from the shadows, rest his chin on my shoulder. Oh yes, ⋯ ⋯ the sawdust under our feet in those good old days. And I ⋯ ⋯or sure somebody had to save me, for here I was in New Y⋯ ⋯ew York, and I wasn't even having fun, couldn't even go fo⋯ ⋯nt drink. Sunday afternoons I spent in Washington Square ⋯ ⋯atching city kids in scuba masks and flippers explore the b⋯ ⋯ths of the three-foot fountain while I ate my Good Humor bar. ⋯ ⋯etimes I went swimming at the Carmine Street swimming pool, where all the sleek lovelies stretched out on the rough concrete like numbers on some celestial clock.

One Friday night I was sitting on my chipped kitchen chair in my living-dining-kitchen wondering what to eat next when I heard a knock at my door. Only one person in the whole world knew where I lived.

That weekend we only went out for food and air. That was the time he told me about the P.O., Saturday baths, and the statue of the Confederate colonel in the town square. I told him that as kids my sister and I jumped on our bed until it broke and then we slept in a heap at a slant until one of my mother's boyfriends tied it up again with twine.

"Those chaotic days are over," he said. I wasn't sure what he meant, what new regime was in store for me, and I had never thought of my childhood as particularly chaotic, just fun. But I did think better of telling him about the time my mother, my sister and I drove through Mexico, the time we picked up a hitchhiker who dropped dead in the back seat of our car. When we drove back to the little seaside town near Ensenada where we had picked him up nobody knew him, wanted to claim him, so we buried him ourselves on a promontory overlooking the beach. We made a cross, since we figured everybody in Mexico was a Catholic, and my sister said a few words just as she had when Stravinsky, our pet beagle, died.

Coming home from work on Monday after our weekend, knowing that Marcus was waiting for me in the apartment, and watching the other working people in the subway with their bags of groceries, tired feet, I felt that at long last I had joined the human race, the real people. I was also going home, had my own bag of groceries and a bouquet of daisies for Marcus, who after all was from the country. Climbing the stairs to the apartment, I expected the door to be open but, from down the hallway, could see that not only was it closed but that somebody had pasted something to the door. At a distance, it looked like the Declaration of Independence, with lots of fancy signatures on it. Up close, I could see that it was a petition and eviction notice. All the mothers of the building, not the Ritz by any stretch of the imagination, alleged that I was a prostitute. Quietly, I unglued the document, stuffed it in my purse, and went inside. Marcus was packing, not because of the sign, which apparently he hadn't seen, but because he had to go back to Virginia, return to his job as a janitor.

At the train station, Marcus said, "I've been accepted at Howard Medical School." People were looking at us standing together, and this was New York.

"I love you, Marcus." I thought I should set the record straight. It was true. I had all the symptoms. Dry throat, clammy hands, etc.

"Do you think we should get married?" he said.

"I don't know." But I wasn't shocked at the idea. Love in my book did not necessarily mean marriage, but I was vaguely aware, even then, that Marcus's book was different. And I also knew, given the world, we had to be serious, all or nothing.

"I have GI benefits," he said. "Also, I've saved. It's been proven that married men do better in medical school than single ones."

"I would work, too."

"Until I finish," he added.

Marriage *was* a thought. After a rather haphazard upbringing, I had gone to a girl's college where everybody on my floor was engaged by senior year. Alumnae notes were full of tidbits about illustrious husbands and accomplished children. Marriage with Marcus would not be tame and ordinary. It might very well be the grandest adventure of all. I could see myself plucking burning crosses from our front yard with my bare hands. Insults from ignoramuses would bounce off my strong chest. I would be a moral Paul Bunyan, showing them all, showing myself. It would certainly be better than living alone in New York, or whatever else I could think of at the moment.

☆   A Baptist preacher married us in Washington. Miscegenation was illegal in Virginia, and we didn't have the money for California. Marcus's former roommate stood up for us, looking zonked out of his mind. I laughed through the ceremony—cosmic joy, I told Marcus, who was miffed. I wore a paisley dress my mother had done up in a hurry, sent off. It was from an Indian bedspread, a pattern on the bottom of orange elephants trekking East. On my long yellow hair, I wore a wreath of laurels. Marcus was in his three-piecer, the one he wore for interviews and on Sundays for church.

Our bedroom overlooked a wonderful tree, and toward November the yellow leaves plastered themselves to the window like large, yellow hands, splayed fingers. They made me think of children's drawings of fall you see in school windows, and yes, I wanted children, a whole slew of them. They would be beautiful, brown Gauguins and I would be the Pied Piper leading them along the beach. Not Virginia Beach, natch. But some beach, somewhere. Marcus wanted two children, a boy and a girl, after he had finished medical school, his internship and residency.

November and the afternoons turned very dark. I'd come home from my job at the *Post* to find a hallway of little girls waiting for their piano lessons in Mary Janes and braids so tight their eyes would slant up. On Saturdays, when Marcus was studying in the library, I swept the leaves off the front porch, helped the Trakleds put in storm windows, learned how to make sweet potato pie and Mississippi mud cake. I took the Reverend's damp tobacco wads, lined up on the porch banister, inside. They looked like frozen bonbons. When Marcus came home he'd shower for hours it seemed, eat quickly, and then fall into bed, tucking up into a tight ball like small armored bugs who curl closed at a touch. My job in the newspaper morgue, where I clipped and filed stories all day, was more tedious than the china shop. At least there I had the Puerto Ricans, the homesick Argentinean. In the morgue, we were all disgruntled history majors, English majors. It was the bookstore all over again.

Around Christmas, Marcus and I were invited to a party. Finally, I was going to meet his study group, talk to some folks. Remembering my mother's parties featuring wine, good talk, I dressed in comfortable slacks, a bulky sweater and my long scarf of many colors. I was prepared to spend the evening on the floor arguing about Marxism, music, Richard Nixon. Marcus wore his suit, as always. Marcus was Marcus. Cuddling up to him on the streetcar going down Georgia Avenue, I thought of when we would be coming home that night. We'd be a little tipsy. It would be like New York again, that weekend, our courtship. But he inched over ever so slightly.

"Anymore and you'll be out the window," I said.

"Joanna."

"I know." He hated public displays of affection, considered them in bad taste. I moved back to my side. The trolley jiggled and jangled, careened around corners. (The tracks are all dug up now. And the trolleys are in museums.) I looked ahead. Washington at night was empty. You could not tell what part of the city was segregated except in terms of buildings. There were good buildings and bad buildings, those with doormen, those without.

"I'm thinking of taking some courses again," I said. "At night, when you're not home."

He didn't catch the hint.

"More history?"

"I won't make that mistake again. Maybe psychology." I knew what he thought of psychology. Not much.

"I'm going to have a lot of papers next semester," he said.

"Meaning?"

"I was hoping you could help type them."

"Ah." But we had arrived. We got off the trolley, crossed the street, entered a dingy, unkept building.

When the apartment door was opened, though, I could see that I was way out of my depth. All the furniture was creamy white, soft and modern. Huge baskets of ferns hung from the ceiling. The lighting was subdued, the music jazz—cool, subtle jazz. The drinks were not jug wine, paper cups, that sort of thing, but a full bar, J&B, a real bartender in uniform, obviously hired for the occasion. People were drinking martinis. The hors d'oeuvres, while not plentiful, were hot, complicated, on silver trays. But the very worst part was that everybody except me was dressed to the teeth in clothes with style and cut, the kind of thing you see in fashion magazines. Marcus should have warned me. I wished I could have just fainted right there on the spot so that

I could be removed, on a stretcher, with a blanket thrown over my body. My only claim to class at the moment was my hair, which was the color of gold, and Marcus, but when I turned he was not there. He had vanished into the crowd.

"Scotch on the rocks," I requested of the bartender.

"Hello there," a voice said behind me. I turned around. The woman was in a sarong-like dress, pleated at the hips. The drape was perfect and the color was shades of green.

"My name is Casey," she said.

"Joanna." Her hair was in a Billy Holiday upsweep, but, instead of a gardenia, she wore a spray of mistletoe over her ear.

"I'm Marcus's wife." She would know Marcus, surely.

"I know." Her complexion and smile were reminiscent of Lena Horne. I couldn't believe this glamorous lady deemed me worthy of a conversation.

"What I've been wondering," and she arched her penciled eyebrows, "is don't they have men where you come from?"

I looked about in a panic searching for rescue, comfort, something, realized I was very much on my own.

"Excuse me, Casey." I was trying hard to hold the tears, keep some semblance of dignity. "I feel sick," I said.

"Then I ducked into the bathroom," I told Mrs. Trakled the next day over tea, candied violets. "I wanted to stay in there forever."

"Oh," Mrs. Trakled huffed. "Those high-brown Louisiana girls think they are something. Just jealous is all. Just jealous."

Mrs. Trakled's relatives looked down on us from their oval frames. They lined the dining room wall, daguerreotypes, in high-collared dresses, watch chains, struck poses. There was nothing of the Reverend, no trace to the past. Sometimes I thought of him spawned spontaneously in some backwoods swamps, a Mississippi grub, pale and translucent, turning in a single lifetime from worm to man, cell to angel. Actually, Mrs. Trakled told me, he had been a preacher doing revivals when she met him. She was called in when the white pianist failed to appear.

"Do you think I should tell Marcus?" I hadn't. Not a word.

"Good heavens, no. Don't tell him a thing."

That night Marcus and I were seated across from each, a late dinner, eight o'clock. I had the oven on and open for added warmth. The wind was whistling outside, and our bedroom windows were freezing up on the inside.

"Sometimes I wish I was in Caifornia, Marcus. Both of us."

"You act like it's my fault you're not." He folded his napkin.

"No I don't."

"Yes you do."

"Like hell I do." It slipped out.

"I hate vulgarity in a woman." I knew he did.

"I hate cruelty in a man," I replied.

"Oh, you people." He sighed, stood up.

"What people are you referring to, Marcus? California people? Other people? White people? For your information, I am *your* people."

"Joanna, what are you talking about?" He sat down again.

"Attitude. Yours."

"You are the one with an attitude."

"I am the one with a sense of family, the only one. Marcus, we are kin. You can't say, 'Oh, you people' to me. It makes you sound like that woman at the party."

"What woman?" He got up, leaned against the sink.

"The one who asked me if there weren't any men where I came from."

"Who said that?"

"Casey."

"She didn't mean anything."

"She meant plenty. Don't defend her. It was a mean thing to say."

"It didn't kill you, did it?"

"That's even meaner. Whose side are you on?"

He sat down, looked absolutely disgusted with me.

"I take you to a party," he said wearily. "I thought you would like it."

"I hated it."

"Great, that's just great."

I picked up his dish, took it to the sink.

"You know, Joanna, those are my friends, the people who help me, the people who would help you. If anything happened . . ."

"Marcus," I turned around from the sink. "Those people would not help me off the sidewalk if I was dying and you know it."

"So what about your friends? Tell me, what they would do for me?"

"My friends don't live in Washington," I said meekly.

"Where *do* they live, Joanna? Anywhere on earth?"

I couldn't tell him what people at work said when I showed them pictures of my husband. I hadn't even told him about my experiences in looking for an apartment. He didn't know what had happened to my world, that is it was more than divided, that it had simply fallen away.

"I didn't see your mother sending us any wedding presents," he continued, "or your sister."

"My mother made my wedding dress."

"That Halloween costume?"

I had to sit down at that. "At least my mother congratulated me," I offered. "Congratulated *us*, which is more much more than your mother did. Remember your mother's letter, Marcus? And I quote: Are you doing the right thing, Marcus? Unquote. She thought I was pregnant or something."

"You could have been. Easily."

"I'll let that go. The point is that you side with the woman at the party."

"There is a serious shortage of Negro men, so that when a white woman . . ."

"Has one of their own . . ."

"Do you know what people think of you, of me, Joanna?"

"Do *you* know? Anyway, I don't care what people think."

"I do."

"You care too much, that's your problem."

"We have to live in society."

"We are society, Marcus." I felt strong enough to get up again, start the dishes. Usually I let them soak, but Marcus recently had explained to me how unsanitary that was.

"The world out there, Marcus, is full of hypocrites and chickenshits."

"It doesn't solve anything to say that."

"It puts it in perspective, Marcus, lets us know what is important, that we are more important." I looked over at him, remembering how I had felt that first time in New York when I opened my door to him. It was instant recognition, as if my door was really a mirror I was looking into. I had felt that close. Now, looking at Marcus, I felt a chill go through me, and it was like being confronted with a blank wall.

"When I become a doctor, Joanna . . ."

"The world will stop."

"You can make fun of it if you want. But do you know what one of my professors told me? He said that when he was doing his internship in a big-city hospital, a northern city hospital, a woman came into the emergency room bleeding to death, but she would not let him stick a needle for a transfusion into her. She would rather bleed to death."

"Did she?"

"No, of course not. He got a nurse to do it."

I sat back down in the chair, put my head in my hands. I knew what was coming. "Tell me about Charles Drew, Marcus, isn't he the one, the one who discovered blood types and then bled to death on some southern road because the nearest hospital was white? Tell me all the stories, tell me all about it."

"You act like those things don't matter."

"I know they do, but *I* am not your enemy. And you can't play it both ways." The wind rattled the windows. "You seem to *be* like the woman at the party, like your mother, people who are outside but want to be inside, yet you hate the inside."

"And you?"

"I am an outsider, too, can't you see that?"

"No. If so, by choice."

"It's not just color, race." I felt outside of everything at that moment. But from my distance I could see that to Marcus I was an insider and that maybe it had been part of my attraction, and that I had taken him for an outsider, but that really in his heart he wasn't. "I'm on the fringe of things, Marcus, of all things, of your things, too; you should be proud of me. I need some company, can't you tell?"

The bare limbs of the tree were scratching against the window like skeleton hands trying to gain entrance. I looked down at Marcus's elegant hand, the one that would cut and snip, sew back up. Formaldehyde from anatomy lab had pinched up the little pads at the end of the fingertips. His knuckles were wrinkled. With a surge of affection, I reached for it. But Marcus drew his hand back.

"For God's sake, Marcus, I don't want to cut it off."

Yet I felt like it suddenly. I could have. Instead, I ran into the bathroom and with two big swipes, using the scissors brought all the way from California, I cut off two feet of my hair, which had taken me since junior high to grow. Then I marched back into the kitchen.

"See," I shouted, putting a fistful of hair before him. "A hair sandwich, how do you like them apples? See what you made me do? Happy now?"

"Joanna." He shook his head as if I was beyond all hope.

"I present you my hair." I tried to make it sound victorious, but my voice began to wobble and my whole body was shaking. Lying there on the table, my hair looked like a prone animal, like a complete supplicant, a totally defeated, dead beast.

"You are so crazy, Joanna. You make everything so damned hard."

"You make it impossible." I was feeling light-headed as if, like Samson, my strength resided in my hair. My neck felt cold, naked; my face was exposed. I was out there, stripped. Like a collaborator.

"You don't care," I wailed. "You don't even care."

"Shh," he said, putting a finger to his lips, but not rising from his chair to hug and soothe me. "You'll wake the Trakleds."

I wailed all the louder. A line of roaches sneaked out from the crack by the side of the table, took note, waved their antennae.

"Shut up, Joanna."

Then I really let loose, and in a few seconds there was a light tapping at the door.

"Joanna, honey, it is I, Matilda Trakled, are you all right?"

I went to the door, opened it a little.

"Mrs. Trakled."

"Oh child, you've gone and cut your beautiful hair, your crowning glory."

"No, it's all right," I said, sniffing. "Your hair is short, Mrs. Trakled."

"That's different. I'm an old woman."

"No you're not." I noticed that her bathrobe, like all her clothes, was a variation on violet.

"Do you want to come down and watch wrestling on TV? Gorgeous George is on."

Gorgeous George was our mutual favorite. Nights when Marcus was not home and the Reverend retired early, Mrs. Trakled and I stayed up for wrestling and mint juleps.

"Maybe some other time." I closed the door gently.

"Toodle-oo," she called, descending the stairs.

"You woke them up," Marcus accused.

"They were up." I looked at the African violet on top of the fridge. It was a gift from Mrs. Trakled, part of her collection, which she kept on a white teacart. Music was her vocation, she explained to me, and horticulture her avocation.

"You've wakened them," Marcus persisted. "Two innocent people."

"They are not that innocent, Marcus." In fact, Mrs. Trakled told me that the Reverend liked to put a pillow under her hips, hike her up. And during the train trip north, he bribed the porter and he and Mrs. Trakled, then Miss Gibson, got together on one of the top bunks in the Pullman. It was a metaphysical experience, I said to myself, their double-decker coupling, a preacher and his accompanist.

"You know, Joanna, I sometimes wonder," Marcus said.

"Me too. I wonder too, Marcus. Tell me." He had never said it, not once, not on our wedding night, never. "Tell me, honestly, do you love me?"

There was a moment of silence between us, a long moment, too long. I could hear the tree scraping and skittling along the baseboards, the roaches, lots of them, or mice. Another moment passed. I thought I could hear the plants on top of the fridge growing or at least straining towards us, its petals attuned to nuance, all hairs standing straight up. Then Marcus cleared his throat.

"Well?" I was waiting. That was it.

"I married you, didn't I?" he said.

He looked up at me, for I was still standing, and I read such fear in his eyes that I wanted to comfort him, tell him it was all right. Because I knew then that there was no point, that it was all over.

Best Minds ☆

Out of our group in high school, Sid was the prima donna. Blonde, willowy, she penned effortless essays in green ink, wore beatnik black, was pale as a kabuki, and spoke of suicide daily. Chunky, I made holes in my papers from too much erasing. When Mr. Whittaker, our English teacher, asked Sidney whom she was seeing for that chronic cough, Sid answered demurely, "Jim Beam." It was the end of the fifties and our high school was on the edge of South San Francisco. Sidney carried a copy of *Naked Lunch* in her woven Peruvian purse, and was not going to college.

College, good job, marriage, evenly spaced kids, that was the itinerary planned for me, and armed with Social Security Benefits and a small scholarship, I was shipped off to the East Coast. Relieved of the necessity of being like cool, I settled in, became one of those people who hang around campus yearlong, working switchboard, painting cafeteria chairs in the summer, and dishing out oatmeal, snatching trays off conveyor belts in the winter. I ended up with good grades, a circle of friends, kids like myself who organized the cafeteria workers, handed out leaflets, and wore jackets too short, scarves too long, and no gloves.

Then after four years, I found myself going home the slowest way possible, Greyhound, the old metal ship of the desert, with cargoes of grandmothers going downstate in flowered chintz, crew-cut boys on leave, stopping in stations of sitting-up sleepers, gobbling down sandwiches of Wonder White, three days, three nights, all out Saan Francis-co.

"You've lost weight," my mother said.

"Only thirty pounds."

She looked about a hundred years old. She had dyed her iron-gray helmet a Jean Harlow white.

"Fixed up your new room," she said.

I could imagine. She had moved out of South San Francisco to a new apartment in a rather ritzy section by U.C. Hospital. I came home to art deco with filmy curtains, glossy furniture. In the back, though, she had a little wooden deck. Behind it rose a hill of eucalyptus trees, the leaves pungent and shiny, the bark a burnt red. A cloth Chinese fish hung on the clothesline. Wind chimes tinkled forlornly. I had forgotten how lonely and chilly the town could be in the early summer, and I was instantly homesick for college.

"Kept all your things," my mother said, ushering me into a veritable shrine to my youth, a museum of artifacts—frazzled pompons (Go Zebras, Go), a collection of animal scatter pins fastened to velvet and, of course, my yearbooks.

"Where's the eternal flame, Mom?"

"Thought you'd like your new room, Lauren."

"I do, I do." Sitting down on the bed, I took out my last high-school yearbook, opened it up. There we were, Sidney Miller, President of the International Club, and Lauren Berg, Vice Pres. Sidney looked great as usual in her black turtleneck, tight skirt, ballerina slippers. "Slated to Succeed" was her caption on the graduation page. I looked like a stuffed woodchuck in my matching sweater set, string of pearls and pleated skirt. "Hard Worker."

"Have you heard anything about Sidney?" I was afraid to ask.

"At Berkeley, where else?" So she *had* gone to college.

"A graduate student?"

"Are you kidding?" My mother seemed to take great satisfaction in telling me, "Married, tied down, two little kids."

"Ah." The right thing in the wrong order invalidated success in my mother's book, yet even I was surprised. I couldn't imagine free spirit, *femme fatale* Sidney Miller married. We used to make fun of the shackles of matrimony as we circled the school grounds, picking out interesting boys. Matching appliances? Not for us. In my case, I secretly feared nobody would ever ask me, so why get my hopes up? And Sidney favored wild, bohemian love affairs. However, if she had married, it was chic, one-upmanship. On her it would look good.

"Do you know her new last name?"

"Singer," my mother spat out. "I hear he was kicked out of Antioch, a real nogoodnik."

☆ "We live in married-student housing." Amazingly, their number was in the East Bay phonebook. Her voice was the same—drifty, classy.

Married-student housing was a cluster of tan, green-roofed barracks. Sidney's apartment was on the second floor of one of them, and, when she opened the door and stepped out, I reached for a hug, a big kiss on the mouth, but she turned ever so slightly, so it was only a cheek I got. Behind her loomed a man, the husband.

"So this is the great Lauren," he leered.

"You've changed," Sid said.

I could have said the same, except that I had gotten thin and she had thickened out. In high school Sid was a Degas ballerina or a debauched Toulouse-Lautrec. Now her face had spread, smoothed, gone pasty. She had grown up and old in one jump. Yet she was still lovely in her new way, and the two little kids, blond bangs, California brown, were gorgeous, and the husband—rangy, hard-jawed, corkscrew curls, poker-chip eyes, Mark Twain mustache—was a looker, a catch.

Dinner was a work of art. Sidney made the bread we ate, the apple butter we spread; the yogurt we spooned was from her own culture. The soup was from her own stock, just the way the French do it. She had embroidered the tablecloth, done unicorns and rainbows on Jeff's blue shirt and the kids' peasant smocks. The whole rickety apartment was color-coordinated and *House Beautiful* in a rustic, budget-conscious California way.

Jeff let me know right away that he didn't have time for small talk. Studying for the Ph.D. in English Lit. was no small potatoes, he would have me know. Latin, Greek, French, you name it; this was scholarship, baby. The whole point from hors d'oeuvres to homemade rhubarb pie was the first-person singular. And Sidney? She was subdued, cowed, certainly not the old Sid I knew and envied. Not the Sidney who penned effortless essays in green ink.

After dinner, little Lauren (yes) and little Jeff sang a stirring rendition with their dad of "Do You Know the Muffin Man?" and then Sidney put them to bed. This involved back rubs, stories, drinks of water while Jeff took out some grass from an old coffee tin and, stuffing his clay pipe, looked over at me. I quickly downed my third glass of Gallo.

"The dynamic duo, I understand," he said. "Eager Beaver and Miz Frigidaire."

I swallowed, wondered how quickly a cab would come. Sidney had returned, poured out another glass of wine for herself.

"So," Jeff continued, "does our guest think I've always been faithful to Sidney?"

Sidney flinched. "Jeff, not now."

"Why not now? Seize the day."

I got up abruptly, tipping my chair, righting it. Gathering some plates, I started for the kitchen.

"Sidney will do that," Jeff said, taking hold of my wrist.

I peered down at both of them. Sidney had a worn-down, hangdog expression. Jeff was king of the barnyard, cock-a-doddle-doo.

"Excuse me." I withdrew my hand. "The bathroom."

I darted toward the hallway, found myself in a cold, small room with a square window, a cloth stretched over it, not a real curtain, and certainly nothing fringed, tatted or crossstitched. No dense handicrafts, it was as if here Sidney's busy hausfrauing had given out. Or maybe this was her refuge, sanity among the porcelain and pipes, a place she could remember her intellect, could recall herself to herself. It was obviously the only room where she could lock the door. Maybe she read books there in the cool shade. Yet ringing the tub was a line of rubber animals, a bath-time Noah's Ark, two-by-two. Perhaps, after all, Sidney had been like the rest of us, that is, afraid of missing the boat, Sidney of all people.

I cried a little, flushed the toilet, ran the water, and opened the medicine cabinet, had a look. Evidently the whole bloody family was on some kind of prescribed medication.

"Clara, Kim, Susan . . ." Sidney was rattling off the names of Jeff's whole teaching section, as I sat down.

"You haven't even mentioned the men," he told her.

"It's Tony," Sidney said. "Isn't it?"

"My mother is a cutter now." I said this too quickly and loudly.

"A cutter?"

I was flailing about for subjects, distractions. My mother, ready victim, offered herself, but as I spoke I realized that I was proud of her.

"She started at sixteen in the rag trade as a sewing-machine operator, paid by the piece, sewing sleeves all day in a tiny Chinatown sweatshop. She moved on to other factories, going from sleeves to legs, finally getting to make whole samples. When my father died, my mother inherited his cutting tools, his contacts."

Tiny, hunchbacked, dwarfed by the long, high cutting table, the cutting knife really a great saw to buzz through the tall stacks of chalk-marked cloth, my mother made it, succeeded. Sidney's mother was a faded, neurasthenic beauty who was never seen out of her bathrobe. Sidney's father was a high-school teacher. What a waste, Sidney used to say of him while she was still in high school.

"It's getting late," I concluded. "My mother will be worried."

I knew that was true. She was probably fretting while watching an oldie on television, something with Leslie Howard in it.

"And so you are visiting home for just a little while?"

"No, Jeff, I'm going to continue school here."

"M.A.?" I knew what he had in mind. Something to keep me busy until, something to fall back on, pin money, a mattress.

"I'm going to medical school at U.C." I knew as I said it that it sounded crass and show-offy, but it was true.

"A little thing like you?"

"No size requirement, Jeff."

Sidney was looking down, her hands playing with the knots under the tablecloth.

"Sidney, have you considered that when the kids get bigger that you could return to school, that . . ."

Jeff's hand skittered across the table, handcuffed my wrist.

"Would you consider sleeping with me, Lauren?"

A kid stirred in his sleep

"I think I hear little Lauren." Sidney fled down the hall. "Cut it out, Jeff," I said. "I've had enough."

He kept his grip.

"This is really stupid, dumb." But his finger was inching along my veins. He didn't blink. It was one of those eerie moments when things slow down, become excruciatingly significant. "Jeff, please stop." I could hear Sidney cooing in the next room, or was it crying? I could see a drop of sweat roll down Jeff's cheek. Everything was in extreme focus, pointed as an arrow. I lost sense of myself. I was no longer the daughter of working-class emigrants, the good girl who had braided up her hair and gone to college, the young woman who had lost blobby white fat along railway platforms, subway stops, no longer the faithful friend, dutiful daughter, comer-from-behind. I gave Jeff an appraising look and wondered exactly what he had in mind—a trio, a duet, something exotic, turns, sisters and brothers under the covers? I could relax, stop trying so hard, it would be easy, so easy. Slowly, I unloosened his hand from my wrist, exposed the soft palm, and he smiled at me as I lifted it to my mouth. I stuck the tip of my tongue out. Oh, he was watching all right. He liked it. It was a treat. I slid my tongue along his palm, opened my mouth wide, wider, and bit down hard.

"You bit me." He whipped his hand away. "Emasculating bitch," he roared, rushing to the bathroom.

"You might need a rabies shot," I shouted back, laughing.

I heard the water running in the bathroom and kitchen, picked up my plate. Sidney was weeping over the dirty dishes.

"Think I'll call a cab, Sid. Thanks for dinner."

"Oh, Laur, I'm so sorry. I wanted it to be perfect."

"It was, in its way." I put my arm around her. "Listen, are you all right?"

"I'm used to it."

"I bet you are."

"He's really harmless, Laur; it's just talk."

"Oh, is that all it is?"

I was exhausted, wanted to be home with the dull buzz of the TV in the next room. But there was old Jeff, the devil himself, standing in the doorway, a handkerchief wrapped around his hand as if he had been grazed in a gunfight. All the theatrics, I thought, without the tube.

"I'll take Lauren home," Sidney said.

"Sid, baby, you know I was just kidding."

"Could have fooled me," I answered for her. "My kingdom for a taxi."

"A taxi would cost a fortune from here, Laur. I'll take you."

"Does anybody care if I'm wounded?" He was actually sniffing.

"Let me see the little hand," Sidney lisped, baby talk. She unwound the handkerchief and kissed the hand, making it well again.

"I was kidding, babe." He gently butted his head against hers.

"I know, Jeffy, I know."

He was not *just* kidding, I wanted to scream. But in that configuration, I was the villain, no doubt, even though he had called me an emasculating bitch, the worst in the book. I wished there was some handy term for the way he made *me* feel, some horrendous insult in the feminine lexicon—the lobotomizing monster.

☆ "You hurt his pride," Sidney said, driving me home.

"Yeah, I hurt his pride all right. Where it lives."

"He *is* my husband, Laur."

Good for you, I wanted to say. Good for your misplaced loyalty. Not my idea of a funny valentine, although I did remember that for one split second, my loyalty was misplaced and I actually found him attractive. But it was like old times, Sidney and I barreling along, the fog, hoops of it entangling the Bay Bridge.

"You probably want to know what it's all about, huh?"

"That's okay." I was hunting for stars, constellations.

"I want to tell you." The oil cans in the trunk of their battered Renault rattled ominously. Actually, I was surprised that Jeff "let" Sidney drive me home.

"You're going to be working at U.C. Hospital, right? Walking around in your doctor coat, clipboard. You know, I checked in there once. Psychiatric. Just the weekend. It was kind of like going to a hotel, a rest."

"Whose idea, and why?" In profile, in the shadows of the car, Sidney looked like her old self.

"It was kind of mutual. Jeff was taking his comps and I was driving him crazy."

"Yeah, and who gets to go to the hospital?"

But she was smiling. It was an adventure, apparently.

"You see, Laur, I did start school. He was my teacher."

"Jeff?"

"No, I met Jeff at the City Lights Bookstore."

"Spare me." We used to hang out there together, hoping to meet a real poet.

"It was Mr. Marcel, and after I was married. I was in his class and he kept looking at me, you see."

"He was French?"

"God, I don't know. He was a man and he was looking at me. After you've been married for three years and have two little kids and a man looks at you, it's enough."

"It is?" For me it wouldn't have been anything. But I could remember when men looking at Sidney was the air she breathed. Essential, elemental, prerequisite.

"Why did you marry Jeff?"

We had crossed the bridge and were in the city now, around Mission. It was gloomy and damp, a stiff little wind was blowing.

"I was pregnant and we were in love."

I couldn't argue with that, although I had figured Sidney for a quickie abortion in Tijuana between dog races and bullfights. It was the pre-Pill world of coat hangers and kitchen tables. One could get frantic over a missed period, or dead. I had a close call myself. My one love affair had taken place in college on a bed raised to the ceiling on stilts, his drum set housed underneath. Here we are on cloud nine, he used to say. Coming down to earth meant him holding my douche bag while I squirted up in his tin bathtub. Real romantic.

"Do you have heat in this car, Sid?"

"It's broken."

We also had to stop and pour in some oil.

"Mr. Marcel wasn't a big deal," she continued when we got back in the car. "He was just an escape hatch, and it wasn't that I didn't love the daylights out of Jeffy, but he was on campus every day with the coeds, and this was my first time out in years. Well, when I told him all hell broke loose."

"You told him?"

"He didn't believe it at first."

"But you convinced him?" Even I knew better than that, yet I could see that telling him was perhaps the whole point.

"He couldn't understand how I could do this to him."

"You're human, Sidney." I was thinking that Jeff might not be the complete devil I had taken him for.

"But to him, Lauren, doing this to him."

"He's human, too, Sidney, not a god."

We were going up hills now. The car chugged and sputtered.

"Betraying him, Lauren, put back his whole academic career."

"Not to mention yours."

"For a man it's different."

"So we've been taught."

We were slipping along the cable-car tracks now.

"We went to somebody, a shrink, and I said the magic words. I said I wanted to kill myself. I did, too, at least a little bit." She let go of the wheel, held up her fingers an inch.

"It's not funny, Sid. Don't play with that."

Although she always had, all through high school. I remember a party we went to in Berkeley and, when the cops came, we, the only high-school kids, had to hide out on the roof, lying very still, face down on the little bits of gravel pockmarking our cheeks. Let's jump, Sidney had said, for a moment meaning it. I knew she meant it.

"The nurses wore regular clothes and there was a living room and a music room and all that junk like it was the most normal thing in the world to be in that ward. But you couldn't get out." She grabbed my wrist, looked in my eyes, just as her husband had done. "Everybody smoked like a fiend and had dope smuggled in in their toothpaste. There was this kid who could play wonderful gospel music, and we all gathered around the piano like it was old home week and he didn't have big, white bandages around his wrists. When Mr. Marcel visited, we wanted to go outside for a walk and got stopped. That's when I knew I couldn't go beyond the nurses' station."

"Mr. Marcel visited?" We were almost at my mother's house.

"In the morning. Jeff visited at night. The kids, you know."

"Here we are, Sidney. You want some coffee, tea?"

"No." Sidney's buttercup face, illuminated by the streetlight, seemed guileless. "I'm getting to the good part, Laur, but first the scary part."

"It's all scary."

"There was a woman there in a housecoat, fuzzy slippers, and she paced the halls all day. You know what happened to her? She had left her husband years ago and was never the same."

I saw a curtain jerk back, fall forward. Ever vigilant, my mother was still up, waiting, as I suspected.

"Twenty years before, Lauren, she had left him twenty years before and was never the same."

"Sidney, we are never the same anyway."

"Come on, don't be dense. She had never gotten herself together. *Since that time.*" Her gray-green eyes looked dilated, as if she were a cat in the dark.

"I think the kid with the bandages is scarier." Sidney's own mother walked about in a bathrobe all the time and she was married. Why should that scare Sidney? "Married women go about in bathrobes, slippers. Marriage doesn't save you from yourself."

"It gets harder to meet men when you get older, Laur."

"How old are you, anyway?"

"Twenty-two."

"Me, too. That's not old. We're young as hell, Sidney."

"I feel over the hill." The image of Mrs. Miller again presented itself, her etheral blue bathrobe, a little vague, dusty afternoons, a house full of old rugs, big pillows, blighted dreams.

"You have to make your own life, Sid, whatever it is."

"I know."

She did know. It seemed that her embroidery was part of it, that she had it all sewed up by the looks of her apartment, that she and Jeff got inside of it, the handmade life, the one she made, and traipsed around in it like a stage horse forever at odds with its front and back.

"Would you like to say hello to my mother?"

"She thinks I'm a bad influence on you, Laur. I am, I guess."

"No, you're not."

"The negative example, then. But let me tell you how it ended, my little sojourn, my magic mountain. I know that when check-out time rolls around I won't be going home. The whole weekend passed by, no doctor. Jeff is going to show up with the kids, so you know what?"

"Why wouldn't they let you out?"

"Dangerous to myself and others. The usual. You know how they have the doctor coats hanging up by the nurses' station? Well, new nurses were due on Monday morning, the week shift. They didn't know what I looked like yet. I checked in on a Friday night. So I stole a doctor coat, put it on in the bathroom with the name tag right on it, and the stethoscope, and I walked right out at the right time. They unlocked doors for me right and left. I looked just like a lady doctor."

"Doctor."

"That's what I said."

"And you haven't looked back."

"Well, Jeff has, a lot."

"He'll get over it."

"I don't know. I still have the dream I had as a kid. In it I am always at the back door trying to get into my parent's house. There is a witch or something behind me, catching up, and I knock and knock, and they won't let me in."

"You *are* in."

"You think so? How come I don't feel safe?"

"Have you ever read the story " 'In Dreams Begin Responsibilities' "?

"No."

"Well, Sid, it means you have to take the bull by the horns." I was lying. It was something my mother would say. The story didn't mean that at all. It was about wispy women, fragile men, people like Sidney, people you admire and love despite themselves.

"When you get home," I said, "Jeff will have all the dishes done and the house will be warm and quiet. He is going to get up from the chair where he is reading, moving from the little circle of light to greet you."

My voice was getting softer. It was a fairy tale, a bedtime story, guaranteed. "He is going to put his arm around you, and you are going to put your arm around his waist and rest your head on his shoulder and he will guide you to your bedroom. The children will be fast asleep and you will hear their steady breathing. You will put on your nightgown. He will tell you, 'Sidney, you are beautiful. I love you. I love you forever.' You will be safe, warm, happy."

☆ The Cat Woman and the Frog Prince

Emma had not been divorced long when she met Rick. At the beginning of her divorced state she had been utterly miserable. Even approaching divorce, there had always been something, if only fights, with her husband, Shelby. Pain, at least. Alone, Emma at first thought of herself as suspended in one of those soundproof, see-nothing, smell-nothing tub chambers, a back-to-the-womb numbness. But as time went by, sensation returned and she began to settle into her single state. She became aware of certain advantages. For instance, Shelby had always been a stickler for order. He was meticulous, delicately aware of dust. Without him, Emma was able to let Rudolph the Red-Nosed Reindeer stay on the roof through Valentine's Day, on into spring, summer and, naturally, autumn. The red worn off his nose, he looked at once woodsy, sporty, continuously seasonal. Emma also permitted the two guinea pigs to live over the toilet, their pellets plinging down through the cubed holes of their cage to the still water beneath. (Life over the Abyss, she explained to literary friends, few and far between.) Moreover, she and the kids, Teddy and Karen, ate buffet-style around the two baby grand pianos.

It was this sloppiness, she supposed, and the seven stray cats, which earned her the neighborhood designation of The Cat Woman. She did not mind, for, like an honorary degree, the title permitted her eccentricity with immunity. It did not keep her piano students away. She was very careful in that respect, insisting that they record their lessons and placing shiny stars on a chart hung up on the downstairs bathroom door. And once every four months, she made a big pot of black-bean soup, cleaned the house after a fashion (hiding assorted junk in the upstairs bathtub, curtain drawn), threw out the cats, and invited all the parents for a recital—an inevitable success.

Besides teaching piano, Emma had another job, which she kept a secret. This was her night job in the Sears and Roebuck Credit Department, calling up people delinquent on their bills. She had a set spiel that she was instructed to parrot, and the supervisor could listen in at any time without so much as a click of warning. Yet the calls never turned out according to plan. Instead people told her their troubles, ranging from termites to death itself. Moreover, during those dark, lonely nights in the emptied store, phone at her ear, Emma began to imagine life as only so many spare parts, kitchen curtains, broken sewing machines, abandoned washers, mail-catalogue items, debris strewn across rutted country roads. She did not tell the voices on the other end that Sears always got their man, citing the examples illustrated in orientation—a nabbing via walkie-talkie in a Bolivian tin mine, or the descent of a helicopter at night on an aircraft carrier in the middle of the black Pacific. She merely listened patiently and only at the end of the litany did she venture, in a disguised voice, using a false name, to faintly suggest, delicately hint that a bill be paid. And still there were bad moments, mixed reactions: one man threatened to sledge-hammer his TV before it could be reclaimed; another man, whose wife had charged and left town, asked Emma to marry him on the basis of her voice alone. That disembodied appeal was the closest Emma came to remarriage the year after her divorce, but she realized that she didn't want to come any closer. Just the idea of marriage made her want to pick up a sledge hammer. Not that she didn't admire men. She did. But from a safe distance.

Emma met Rick shortly after the phone proposal at a Mature Singles group called Discovery run by the Unitarian Church. The format of the weekly occasion involved meeting in small groups early in the evening to discuss some aspect of the single state and then a party afterward. The night she met Rick the topic for her group had been change, or, as it was called, passage. The nine men in her group, including the peer leader, all stated variations on the theme that they would never change no matter what, and their divorces, it seemed, had largely been due to some woman, their former wives, not accepting them as they were. The eight women besides Emma, in practically one voice, honestly expressed that they were wondering what their exes were doing Right Now. This Very Minute. Emma could have told them that, as they were suspecting, their exes were out having loads of fun somewhere. She could have told them that if they telephoned an empty apartment they could definitely feel free to imagine the worst. She also could have consoled that they would feel better in time, but that there was nothing to be done, present tense. She figured it took a year. What she actually said when her turn came around was that maybe people did not change, but they had layers that they gradually revealed, so initial appearances might be deceiving. That, she continued, led to a sense of betrayal. It had been that way with her husband, Shelby. At the heart of his being, he was not the person she had married. As usual, nobody understood what she was talking about and she managed to set up a train of confusion. But her peer leader, with four hours of training in group dynamics, was able to guide them all back to calm and quiet, zipping up raw wounds, yanking together loose ends, and completing the session with a bleak, craggy smile, apparently as unchanging as the Dakota hills.

After the discussion groups, the ranks of Discovery filled up. That was when more reticent men arrived, fortified with television sportscasts and drinks on the road. The night Emma met Rick she noticed that there were several Sikh Indian men in turbans, wisps of long black hair showing beneath the knotted cloth, standing near the potato chips. Emma thought they might be married. They were too sleek and self-satisfied to be single—like cats licking their paws after a nice bowl of milk. She recognized some other faces, returnees, people who found somebody for a while, dropped out of the group and then, alone again, reentered. It was called retrenching.

The worst moment for Emma was when the music came on. That was when she had to ask herself what she was doing there, why she had come at all. It was like high school—those panicked occasions in the gym when she had to close her eyes and hope somebody would ask her to dance.

"Do you want to dance?" she asked the man standing next to her, a tall, pale man in a camouflage shirt with his hands in his brown corduroy pants who did not look old enough to be a Mature Single.

"No. I don't dance."

She was taken aback. They usually obliged.

"Why do you come to a dance, then?"

"Really, I don't dance. I never come to these things."

"Neither do I," she said.

"I don't know why I'm here," he went on, not looking at her, but facing out to the dance floor as if contemplating a desert.

"I don't know why I'm here either," she admitted.

"I'm not even here," he finished.

The music was what her kids would call mood music—watered-down Beatles, old fifties tunes jazzed up, dentist-office stuff. The punch bowl was being set out by the president of Mature Singles, Petra Borgen, a weathered, rumpled veteran of many retrenchments.

"She looks like a turtle, don't you think?" The young man nodded toward Petra.

"No, I don't think so. Petra is too vulnerable."

And then he turned to Emma, as if suddenly interested in her, revealing light-green, almost yellow eyes with elongated, oval pupils. He was so tall that he had to hunch down to look at her. She realized that they would have been ridiculous on the dance floor.

"What do you do?" he asked.

"One of those," she said, half to herself.

"Sorry, I didn't catch that."

"I said, 'You are one of those.'"

"One of what?"

"You define people by their occupations. You are how you eat."

"No, I didn't mean it that way. I just didn't know what to say next. I'm new to the Washington area and I find that occupation is the standard entry into a conversation, any conversation."

"Whom do you talk to?"

"Well, my colleagues at the Smithsonian. They're not the ones who ask. People on the subway, mainly."

"I happen to be a piano teacher." Naturally, she left out Sears and Roebuck.

"That's nice."

"It's boring."

"I'm sorry."

"There is nothing you can do about it."

"Are you sure?"

Then silence fell between them.

"Oh shit," she finally said.

"Sorry," he said, "but I'm a little hard of hearing."

"I said, 'Oh shit.'"

"I agree. Do you want to go somewhere else?"

"No."

"Are you divorced?" He asked this facing the dance floor again.

"Yes, thank you, and you?"

"Kind of."

"Married?"

"Oh no. I don't believe in it."

She found that information relieving, somehow.

"Why did you get your divorce?" He was swaying a little as he talked.

"Why?" Nobody had ever asked, assuming, she thought, that any reason was good enough. "I'm a refugee from political oppression," she answered.

"Really?" He put his face close to hers, and she saw that he had small teeth, baby teeth, somewhat gray around the gums. His nose was quite flat, with almost curly nostrils.

"No, not really." She sighed.

"I'm really interested. I want you to tell me."

She doubted that he would want to hear what she had to say. She looked out at the dance floor, which, full of dancers, appeared ordinary, normal.

"Sometimes I think of myself as one of the walking wounded; but that's stupid, isn't it?"

"No," he said. "Anyway, it doesn't show."

"What is your name?" She would tell him the truth, but she had to know his name first.

"Rick McClintock."

"Well, it's very simple, Rick, my marriage. I found out after fifteen years of marriage, two kids, or rather, it was Shelby, my husband, he found out, anyway, he discovered, to him it was gold. . . . What I mean is that he was homosexual. I believe the euphemism is 'gay.' He was gay, Rick, and I was sad."

"Hmm."

She knew he was giving it some thought as he looked away from her face at her flat chest, trousered legs. And yes, she had a short haircut, tweed jacket, string tie.

"You think I'm boyish."

"No, not necessarily. I don't think divisions are very clearcut between the sexes or between animals. I was just thinking that you looked like a small mammal."

"Thanks."

"No offense. I regard all people in that light."

"Sometimes I do, too."

"Like when I'm going underground, on the subway, that is, I can imagine a whole menagerie. I see wolves, birds, fishes, antelopes; and the ones in high heels, scared eyes, those are the antelopes, skittish. It would take so little for all of us to revert back—fur, scales, a little narrowing of the face, darkening of the nose, lengthening of the ears. Now you, you are a nice little field mouse."

"I would rather be a swan." But he didn't appear to hear her.

"You see, I'm a herpetologist."

"Herbs? Herpes?"

"Amphibians, reptiles. My specialty is snakes. We know very little about mating patterns of snakes. I'm doing a postdoc at the Smithsonian."

She had seen a photo once of a small snake eating a large egg, swallowing whole. The idea of such a creature mating was not too appealing.

"It's been very nice talking to you, Rick," she said, backing off.

"I have quite a collection I brought with me."

"To the dance?"

"No, the East Coast." He was following her to the door.

"Live?"

"In bottles."

"You collected them yourself?" She was at the door now.

"From all over the world."

She opened the door. Winter gusted in.

"Listen. Miss . . ."

"Emma."

"Emma, would you like to go out for dinner or something, sometime?"

"Lunch is better. I'm on the telephone a lot at night."

"Lunch then. We could meet in the cafeteria of the Natural History Museum."

She hesitated, pulling in the door a little. The idea of lunch with a man, any man, was frightening. What if she should gag or spill something, dribble, burp? But wasn't that why she came to Discovery, Mature Singles, to get out juvenile fears and learn to live and to do the things people did? She had chronic insomnia at night, and usually slept in the day, rising only in time for afternoon lessons, to get Karen and Teddy home from school. Lunch would give her something to wake up to.

"You know, Rick, the problem is I haven't had such a prolonged conversation with an adult. I mean, face-to-face, in a good while. I have been in a terrible mood lately."

"That's okay, Emma."

"And I don't cook."

"I'll do the cooking, if necessary. I don't see cooking as a stumbling block to a friendship, do you?"

"This group is, if you want to get down to it, therapy for me."

"Me too. No problem. Right now my former roommate's ex-girlfriend, who had moved in with him, with us . . . it's like this. My roommate and I had the apartment first, and then his girlfriend moved in with him, with us, and then they broke up and he moved out. She stayed. She's still there. She thinks I'm moving to Texas, so she's hanging on. In the evenings she tries to outstare me."

"What kind of animal is she?"

"A stork. Very unappetizing, all bones and beak." He smiled.

"Friday, the gift shop at eleven, by the stuffed white tiger?"

"Sure." She opened the door, quickly running to her Volvo, her only inheritance from Shelby besides the house, which she had to pay for, and the two baby grands.

☆ In the daylight at the museum near the blown-up picture of the spider, Emma realized that Rick was handsome, a handsome young man. Wearing the same mottled shirt and brown pants, he had made an attempt at combing back his shaggy blond hair. Patches were still wet, and his small ears were pink, as if he had been outside. They sat in the cafeteria in the midst of anxious mothers and tired children. She had been like that a long time ago, dragging Teddy and Karen to the displays. As teen-agers, they went to the park near the house, where they smoked cigarettes and drank beer. It was better, she supposed, than if they went to the shopping mall and sat on the curb smoking dope, popping pills. At least they were not inhaling exhaust fumes and getting arrested.

"Until my divorce, I had a part-time job playing piano in a dance studio. Then one day I saw my husband dancing with a friend."

"Ballet? At the studio?"

"That's a cliché about ballet dancers." She stretched her neck so she could speak softly across the table. "It was at home, ballroom dancing."

Dancing was a euphemism. As gay was to homosexual, so was dancing to opening the utility closet, finding Shelby and Lins on the dirty-clothes pile. She had closed the door very quickly but, of course, had seen them, no turning back. Lins had earrings in both ears, socks and a watch on. Shelby was in his Beethoven T-shirt. Ever since, Emma had been leery of closet doors and in her own home had removed them, giving the cats easier access to their boxes.

"My husband owned a string of movie houses, tin-can theaters we called them—small, side-by-side, uncomfortable, blurred subtitles. He started with avant-garde, moved to softcore, made a bundle."

"Soft porn?"

"Yes, that's it."

She and Karen had seen *Dear Detective* in one of his theaters after the divorce. *Last Tango* was blaring in the adjacent theatre, and all during *Dear Detective* Emma kept wondering if they had reached the point where Marlon Brando showed his bare bum. The galvanized tin walls separating the theaters seemed to be sweating, running rivulets of tar, and then afterward, waiting under the canopy in front of Theaters I, II, III for the rain to stop so that they could make a run for the car, she and Karen saw a large rat dizzily barrel across the street, heading straight for their feet and only veering off at the last minute to a hole in the wall. It was one of the worst evenings of her life; she had never felt so wretched and unrevenged.

"I was a math major in college," she told Rick, feeling compelled to get off the subject of Shelby. "But I realized that I would probably end up in some insurance office computing mortality and morbidity, cheery stuff, and, since I had enough credits, I graduated in music. I've never looked back."

She smiled. The confession constituted conciliation, whether Rick knew it or not. He sipped his coffee reflectively, bit his nails.

"Do you want to go to the movies?" he said. "Not your husband's, of course. Tomorrow night?"

"I don't know. I mean, this could be a business lunch."

"It wouldn't be a date, if that's what you mean. Two friends go to the movies, that's all."

"Are we friends?"

"We're not enemies."

"No."

"Well then."

The film was *Missing*. About a young American killed in Chile's military coup, it had been out a while, but, looking at the long line of bearded and bejeaned middle-aged people waiting in the line curving around the block in front of the theater, Emma thought that all the radicals in the Washington area had crept out of a ten-year hibernation. Rick said that right after hibernation, coming out of their caves, was when dens of snakes mated.

"Snake orgies," Emma kidded. "In the den, from the pits."

In addition to hawkers of leftist newspapers and solicitors for various petitions, a young woman in a black-and-red plaid jacket and green army fatigues worked up the line, asking people to put down their name and phone number. Universal City Studios, she explained, was doing a survey to find out if people liked the film. Rick told Emma not to sign and, when the young woman was out of hearing, said it was the FBI checking up, not Universal City Studios; indeed, before they got into the theater a car full of kids roared by, all of them shouting, "Commies, go home."

Once the movie started, there was much esprit de corps, with clapping and booing at appropriate moments. It was this, plus the potentiality of danger on the outside, that made Emma feel close enough to Rick to let him hold her hand, high-schoolish as it was. Afterward, though, self-consciousness returned and, rather than going to her house for coffee, she suggested a coffee house, which she found, to her chagrin, full of Mature Singles giving each other the eye across the smoky room.

"My brief foray into politics," she began. "One night I get this hushed, breathless phone call. It is somebody from the Animal Liberation Front." His cappuccino had left a froth of white over his lips. She wanted to wipe it off, but she wondered if, one, it would be too intimate, and, two, it would be too motherly. "A group of Animal Liberators apparently had just broken into some university laboratory and rescued twenty experimental cats. They asked me if I would receive stolen goods; i.e., a cat. That's how I got Belinda, my calico. Is she grateful? No, she is not."

Rick just looked at her.

"Do you think I'm a crank? I have seven cats now. The population is at an all-time low. I don't even like cats."

"I've always loved snakes. You don't need to apologize."

"*Loved* snakes?"

She leaned closer. The shop was decorated like a French sidewalk café. Edith Piaf was the featured artist at high volume. The waiters looked Ethiopian as they wove among the tables. Perhaps they were Americans. She no longer trusted her perceptions.

"God yes, I've loved snakes since I was a kid in Mississippi. When my father took me fishing, I hunted snakes."

Shelby had collected baseball cards.

"You don't have a southern accent."

"I know. I'm the only weird one in my family, the only one to go to college, to come near to going to college. I've run after snakes, swam after them. As an undergraduate I collected for the university museum."

"Do you—did you—wear a snake suit, boots, gloves, protection?"

Shelby wore baseball caps.

"No, I don't wear boots or gloves. I like to feel what I have."

"Even if they're poisonous?"

"Particularly then."

He brushed the bangs out of his eyes, smiled his milky smile. she thought she felt his foot on hers, bare sock, toes inching up her legs, but it turned out to be sheer imagination. She was just too jumpy.

"That girl is sitting in my living room staring up the walls. Otherwise . . ."

"It's all right, Rick, believe me."

The last thing she wanted to do was rush into anything. Her only escapade, not counting the phone proposal, was with a chimney sweep, somebody she did not know, who came when the chimney got too blocked to draw. In his tight black pants, tailcoat, black-and-white striped T-shirt and tall, black top hat, he was immediately impressive. With jaunty, almost playful movements, he placed a huge vacuum tube up the chimney and while it noisily sucked away he had time for a beer. Afterward, a bit sooty, he had to wash up. The kitchen, with its pile of dirty dishes and trays of cat food, did not discourage him and he joined them for dinner à la fresco without a blink of the eye. Conversation and camaraderie in the sack seemed hardly more than the logical extension of hospitality, and fortunately he took it that way, leaving in the morning after frozen pancakes, light and easy, no promises. Teddy and Karen, intent on a Who concert coming up in the Capital Centre, barely noticed, which was not the case with the neighbors. It was the truck, Jiminey Cricket painted on its side, resting innocently in her driveway all night, that proved most offensive. Taxicabs, bread trucks, message bikes, commercial wheels of any kind were vehicles non grata along the highways and byways of genteel Chevy Chase. The dirty looks went on for weeks.

"I don't wear a special suit for snake hunts," Rick was saying, "but I do have a snake stick, with prongs."

Somehow that made Emma think of the devil's pitchfork.

"I used it only once, though, in Ghana," he practically shouted over the rockabilly.

"Maybe we should go," she said. "You can tell me in the car."

His car was a Pinto. He kept the heater on all the time, and he wore a bulky coat, scarf, mittens, earmuffs, enough paraphernalia to go skiing in. A southern boy, educated in California, he no doubt found Washington freezing.

As they wove through town she pointed out the sights. Embassies to the right, slums to the left, that's where the president lives, we are now passing the zoo. It made her think of "The Carnival of the Animals." But Rick would not know music, and she wasn't good at small talk. What could she say to a person she hardly knew, a person that she might never know even after years and years? When she was younger she believed in carnal knowledge, that intimacy was revelatory. Now she knew that you could sleep with a man for fifteen years, watch him eat breakfast, tie his shoes, brush his teeth, see the minutiae of his life, and still know nothing. Sex itself was still another masquerade, another skin shed, more beneath. As far as she was concerned, it was hopeless.

"You traveled on airplanes with your snakes?" She said this facing forward into the darkness, the way he had peered out onto the dance floor that first night, as if perceiving pattern and meaning.

"I usually have a permit, but I've been through customs with hundreds of salamanders hidden in the bottom of my sleeping bag."

That sounded worse than a bag of snakes. She didn't inquire whether Dead or Alive.

"That reminds me, Rick."

"What say?"

"I said, that reminds me of when I went to Girl Scout camp a long time ago. Some kids oiled a stick, stuck it in my sleeping bag.

That was enough for me, the unreasonable facsimile."

"I guess we'll have to do something about that." He raised his mittened hand off the steering wheel, patted her on the shoulder. "Why don't you come backstage, I mean, to the labs at the Smithsonian, where I work. I can show you that there is nothing to be frightened of, nothing at all. Familiarity, you see."

It would be another event. Perhaps Karen and Teddy would like to come, except she was afraid that their presence would be presumptuous. Not like cultural exposure, but rather: This is my boyfriend, the snakeman.

"I like your Bambi," he said, depositing her unharmed at her door.

"It's Rudolph," but he didn't hear, already backing out, and really, if she were honest, the plaster figure with its chipped paint, broken ears, was no longer Rudolph. At night, looming sinisterly, it resembles an ever-vigilant watchdog, and in the day it is only a seedy statue.

That night Emma had bad dreams, a childhood carryover—the chase, the monster, and always waking up in time. Throwing the six cats off her bed, the living, purring, kneading and shedding fur blanket, she padded downstairs for a cup of hot chocolate. Passing through the living room, she noticed Dingaling, her Siamese, licking some Chef Boy-ar-dee spaghetti off the top of one of the pianos. Shelby had bought her those pianos when he started to get rich and before Lins. Man and wife, they were going to do duets. Now those instruments were her bread and butter, she at one, the nervous student at the other. She went into the kitchen to get a rag. The lone bulb revealed a drainboard splotched with stains and the opened fridge presented a baking-soda box fuzzy with mold. Dim movie music wafted up from the basement—a late-night adult film, just what the doctor ordered.

"Turn down the TV," she screamed down the stairs, littered with dirty clothes.

She closed the fridge, went back into the living room to clean the piano. She must do something about the kids, she realized for the hundredth time. Shelby had volunteered to pay for Exeter. Exeter or nothing; only the very best. That was Shelby. But was it the solution? From the ridiculous to the sublime? Punk to prep? She sat down at one of her pianos. When Shelby had left, she first had played Chopin all day, returning again and again to "Prelude 20." It matched her depression, kept her fingers moving, and she could look up, watch the door, where she expected him in a moment, bags in hand, the Swedish summer over. Moving to "Song without Words" by Mendelssohn, she had remembered that Shelby had always been crazy about Bergman films, the moody ambiguity matched with stark interior design. All that blond furniture, all that crap, and her mood changed from hopeful to hateful, while she banged out Beethoven's "Hammerklavier Sonata." That was when the kids started weekend visits to Shelby's new home in Cleveland Park. Visits that did not seem to harrow their souls or rot their teeth. On the contrary, Lins was an expert cook, a magnificent host. During their weekends with their father, they went to bed at a reasonable hour, did not smoke because of Lins's allergies, drank wine only with dinner, took baths, combed their hair, did their homework. Thus Emma was even denied snide remarks about their "stepmother." Shelby and Lins, lover and lover, had settled down into a domesticity both more diverse and intense than she could ever provide. She gave up any effort in that direction, letting first one thing and then another slide until she had to beat a path to the bathroom from each bedroom.

That night, putting down her tomato-stained rag, she began playing Bach, "The Two-Part Inventions." She began slowly, disregarding dynamics, tempo, just getting the notes. But as they began to weave over on top of each other, she found herself reading more closely, crescendoing, making her fingers bounce the counterpoint. For a few minutes, she felt like her old self—the eager math student, the happy young wife, doting mother, careful teacher. And she could picture herself fitting into new slots—the independent woman, the courageous single parent, the older woman—everything neat and trim, exactly as it was suppose to be.

☆   The day Emma visited the Smithsonian was gray and cold. An old man in front of the White House held up a sign: Welcome to the Madhouse. She continued on past the monument, winding around the Smithsonian parking area to find a place in front of the Castle, the old turreted structure that she understood had been the original museum. In order to get into the laboratory section of the Natural History Museum, it was necessary to get a visitor's badge. Rick met her in the marbled lobby by the elephant, guided her through mazelike corridors in back of the displays and up some stairs. They emerged behind the anthropology area and the second floor. Next door to the Amphibians and Reptiles was the Worm Department. It appeared that the two groups shared certain facilities. Their Christmas tree, Emma could see, was mutual. In the middle of the hallway, it sported cutout snakes, turtles, lizards, frogs and various worms.

"That's for you." Rick said, pointing to the lone mammal on the tree, a cat, paws extended, bracing for a fall.

"*Mucho gusto,*" she said.

"*De nada.*" He smiled, bent low, and brushed her with his mouth. There was hardly anybody around.

"Well, Emma, the tour, right? The complete tour?"

She nodded. They were at the library, where a big poster taped to the card catalogue declared: Venomous Toads Patrol These Premises.

"Our humor," he explained.

On top of some of the stacks were snakeskins. There was a snakeskin cane and an old stuffed sea turtle, its eyes glassy, and jars of frogs, which, although dead-looking, had their legs extended as if they were getting ready for the great leap to freedom. On the walls were some maps showing geographical concentrations of various species.

"This is where my boss is measuring the courting songs of frogs," Rick said, opening a door to a lab with a lot of electrical equipment.

"Do snakes court?" Emma asked. "Do they have songs?"

"They don't hear very well, really not at all, not the sound traveling through air waves. They catch vibrations."

"Oh."

"But they have a keen sense of smell."

"Is that so?" She wondered if they tracked their prey, but did not ask.

The labs were the usual, she thought—the black-topped sinks, microscopes, glassware. There were trays and carts full of jars, all filled with frogs or some kind of eggs, small turtles, even small snakes. But somehow they appeared, in their contained condition, to be harmless, like pale meat. She knew, however, that they were slimy; but so were marinated artichoke hearts, her favorite. People ate snails, after all. Furthermore, with the soft winter light filtering through the tall, dusty windows, it was like a university. She felt hushed, in awe, and somewhat bored. Emma had gone to school in the Midwest. She was from Ohio; both her parents were schoolteachers. Shelby was from New York and was brilliant. In the midst of the dull, old buildings, the flat gray skies, he had stood out like a bright, three-dimensional flower. Suddenly for Emma there had been color, noise, life. The first time they made love in his dorm room, the whiteness of his buttocks had startled her. She knew, looking at Rick loping down the hall, that those experiences could never be duplicated. This was a museum, not college, and she felt like a relic.

"Emma, are you with me?"

"Yes, I was thinking I would need to have a recital soon. That means housecleaning."

"Am I invited?"

"Of course." She thought of him towering above the parents and children, flaring his funny nostrils.

"A bit of a misnomer," he mentioned as they passed a door labeled Live Specimens.

There were a few people in their offices, small cubbyholes, little rat nests. Their work looked tedious to her, but Rick, drawing her down the hall, his arm loosely draped over her shoulder, shepherding her with obvious pride, was really in his element.

"We don't have much from Madagascar," he said, pausing in front of a set of double doors, "but otherwise our collection is one of the most complete. We get specimens all the time for classification."

He opened the door. The room was dark and, by feel, vast.

"Let me find the switch." One row of phosphorescent light revealed gray metal library stacks filled with bottles of specimens. "Light makes them fade," Rick explained, "so we only turn on what we need as we go. Some of our stuff dates back to Linnaeus."

They proceed step by step through little strips of light, individual switches at each stack, darkness sealing off the return and the way ahead. They made their way through frogs, lizards, turtles, pink eggs, blue eggs.

"The larger specimens are in metal tanks. We won't open them."

Emma was dizzy by the time they reached the snakes. The way back through the thousands of specimens seemed long, somehow treacherous.

"We should have dropped crumbs," she said softly.

"What?"

"Nothing."

She imagined that they were in the catacombs, in the archives, at the heart of snake scholarship, down finally to the primeval serpent that lay coiled and sleeping. All around them, upstairs and below, she could conjure busy bee workers wrapping mummies, stuffing owls, sewing feathers, while adjacent to them trooped the unending parade of mothers. Rick held up a jar of tangled vipers. Cleopatra's? And where was the head of Medusa in this complete collection? Holmes's speckled band, Hawthorne's guilt? The labels were deceptive. *Vermicella calonota. Micrurus fulvius. Matacora birvirgata. Agkistrodon piscivourous. Agkistrodon contortrix.*

"I'm not scared, Rick," she found herself almost shouting, "but I want to go home."

"I'm glad you're not scared." He had been holding her hand, but now, nearly at the end of the stacks, he stood, facing her, his hands on her shoulders.

"Rick."

"Yes?"

"I think . . ."

"Don't worry about it," he said, bending low; and, first nuzzling her cheek, he kissed her. She felt his tongue flick in, flick out. Her lips stung.

She edged to the end of the light, a little isthmus of yellow. Her brain was clouded. She didn't know how to put it to him. "Rick," she began again. "I feel like I'm in a graveyard, the elephant burial ground—like that. Sorry, I didn't mean it in the way you think. What I want to say is that I'm not ready for an involvement. I don't have the energy. But I like you, really."

"I'm glad you like me, Emma." She could hear him breathing short, raspy breaths.

"Really and truly, Rick. I'm scared."

"Yes, Emma," but, speaking between his breathing, he sounded funny, and swaying above her in the greenish light, among all those jars, it seemed to her that his neck was thickening and his mottled shirt was spreading and that his arms were fusing into his sides, and, although he had told her that snakes did not have courting behavior and could not hear, his whole body appeared to be slowly dancing to some ancient, fluted rhythm rising from the floor, mapping his movements, impelling him, somehow, to come and get her.

☆ *Collect Calls*

Monday night down at the shelter and things are popping. The TV is on to cable and Dr. Ruth is interviewing the Mayflower Madam. When Dr. Ruth says she believes in prostitution, a wild yippee-yi, yippie-yea goes up. When the Mayflower Madam oh so slowly crosses her legs, the guys groan hubba, hubba.

Melinda Ann is at the stove stirring the soup. She is wearing her Palestine scarf, a fake leather skirt with a big slit up the front, and granny glasses. Some volunteers from the local synagogue and the Young Christians are wrestling with the coffee urn. As usual, it's clogged. The radio in the kitchen is on—Paul Simon and the Boyoyo Boys. A reporter and her cameraman from Channel 12 are setting up in one corner. The reporter is none other than Leslie Untaker, anchorwoman *par excellence*, and she is doing a minidoc on the Homeless in America. But something seems to be wrong with the battery pack. All the right numbers are flashing, but no sound is being recorded. One of the synagogue volunteers gives the machine a good smack and, inscrutably, the gizmo jumps into action.

"Cameras are rolling," Leslie announces and, pushing the mike in a guest's face, asks, "Tell us your life story, will you, how you got here, where you came from, what you are about, who you are, and give us a thumbnail of life on the streets. Maury, move in closer."

"Now hold on one minute." Charlene, the site supervisor and a bigwig in the church upstairs, which has donated its basement to the shelter, moves in. "No filming without permission of the person." Upstairs are Charlene's office, the Love Room, Sunday-school classrooms, the general meeting room used by the community groups, in particular one devoted to stopping U.S. aid to the Contras, the main room for services, bathrooms—all topped by a huge dome resembling St. Peter's or a mosque. Actually, it is a Baha'i church.

"It's cool, Charlene, they can film me."

"Just so nobody is messed with, Archie, that's all I care about."

Charlene, maybe three hundred pounds, has been around the block, as she is the first to admit. Before joining the Baha'ists, which she figures was just about the time Tina Turner became a Buddhist, Charlene was an alcoholic. According to the rules of AA, she still is one, although she hasn't taken a sip in years. "You want to know what an alcoholic looks like?" she will ask, thumping her chest like Tarzan. She does this in orientation for volunteers, to show the fine line between staff and guests.

For instance, Melinda, who is doing a Ph.D. in urban studies, has had many bad experiences in her life and says that the field work she is doing at the shelter is close to home. Many of the guests are young men who look like the Young Christians, in their pink button-down shirts, crisp jeans, combed hair. And some of them insist on wearing their knitted caps inside, as if they were perpetually at devotion in their yarmulkes. But there is no mistaking Leslie Untaker, who, tweeded to the gills, could have stepped right out of a Ralph Lauren advert.

"Tell me your life story," she asks again, wetting her lips.

"We in Baha'i believe in the unity of all mankind," Charlene says.

"Personkind," Melinda corrects.

"Who dosen't?" Archie adds.

"It's the idea that if one of us were Jesus," puts in one of the Young Christians, "like if the Messiah were to appear on the street needing a place, could we afford to turn Him away?"

Leslie Untaker, with the mike pointed at Archie, sighs, shakes her head.

"Don't look at me," he says. "I'm a secular humanist."

"Arch is Catholic," Manny mentions. "I'm the atheist."

"Manny, are you really?" Charlene seems surprised.

The cameraman, giving up on Archie, pans around the room.

"Fucking camera," an old man grumbles, "Get it out of my face."

"Gary," Charlene warns. "No bad language."

"Sorry. Frigging camera."

"Gary has a problem," Melinda explains, pushing up her glasses, which keep slipping down her nose. "It comes in a bottle and it's not a prescription."

"I do not have a problem," Gary defends, "I'm just drunk, and I hate to be photographed."

"That's what I mean, Gary."

"You are on the air." Dr. Ruth has gotten to the call-in portion of her program. "Dr. Ruth," the voice begins faintly, "my girlfriend and me. . ."

"I'm going to Graceland/Memphis, Tennessee," Paul Simon croons.

"I didn't catch that." Manny leans toward the TV, all attention. The row of folding chairs is set up in a semicircle so that everybody can see.

"Something about doing it in a hot tub, I think."

Manny gives Melinda the once-over. From Kentucky, she is a tall, rangy woman. "You got a name?" he asks.

"Melinda Ann."

"Ready to roll, rea-dy to roll," Leslie interrupts. "We need to get something we can keep."

"I was put in jail," Archie admits, continuing his life story, "for kissing the elbows and knees of a teen-age girl."

"He has a problem," Manny says, "if I ever heard one."

"Just a little S and M," Melinda explains.

"M and M?" Archie is confused.

"It's hard to get a date after a certain age." Melinda agrees.

"You want to go on a date?" Manny asks Melinda. "I'll take you on a date."

"No thanks, not now." Melinda, though, gives Manny the once-over. Manny wears a Playboy bunny on a chain around his thick neck and a Pittsburgh Steelers cap. "There are a group of us vets," he informs Leslie Untaker, "who live under the bridge. Poor boys, black and white, that's who they sent to the front in Nam. Probably Korea, too. No difference since the world began."

"Whose life story are we doing, anyway?" Archie is miffed.

"The soup is ready," Melinda announces. "You guys want to tape the soup?"

"Tape the damned soup," Leslie says.

"We don't allow bad language around here," Charlene points out. "All I ask is that people read the rules. No weapons, no bottles, no needles, *no bad language*." She is fixing the coffee for everybody, while Melinda hands out the soup from the little window between the kitchen and the main room, where the men eat and sleep. There are about twenty, and seven volunteers. December, the temperature has dipped below zero.

"After that kissing incident," Archie continues, "they put me in a strait jacket, gave me this creepy doctor. He'd carry on. 'What's on your mind, Arch?' 'Nothing, doc.' 'Knock, knock, anybody home?' 'We're all home.' 'Stop that.' 'I'm going to kill you, doc.' 'Oh yeah.' 'Yeah.' 'You know that bad man on the sixth, the one in isolation who killed his grandmother? I'm going to tell him to kill you, Arch.' "

"You call that therapy?"

"Exactly my point, Manny, you took the thoughts right out of my head."

"We also have some pâté," Melinda tells Leslie. "Donated. That I'll smear."

"See, I am the only one who can call the police," Charlene is telling the cameraman, "just in case you were wondering. It used to be the volunteers could, but at the slightest ruckus they were ringing up, and the whole scout troop would be barreling down the stairs, disrupting our evening, tripping up on everything, trying to win their eagle badges. One night they almost wrecked the Love Room."

"Could you tell us a little something about the Love Room?" Leslie Untaker is very interested. The camera zooms in on Charlene.

"Have you ever done it in a bathtub?" Manny asks Melinda.

"I'm not keen on chemicals," she answers, "although, as you can see, I chain-smoke Camels occasionally." Melinda's thin white fingers are edged in nicotine and the little hairs above her lip look tie-dyed in purple. But it only adds to her mystique and charisma. She is obviously a woman of character.

"The Love Room is where you can go to get clothes when you need them," Charlene is saying, "Coats, boots, sweaters, like that."

"Like free love," Manny concludes, arching his eyebrows provocatively at Melinda. "May I call on your father, Melinda?"

"I'm a feminist," she replies.

"So, I'm a humanist," he counters.

"You're lazy."

"Maybe, may-be."

"What happened to me," Archie clears his throat, "is that I lost my whole family, my job, my home, the works. You know how one thing leads to another? A couple of slip-ups is all it takes. I called my family collect after I got out of the hospital and they wouldn't even accept the charges."

"There is a lot of hurt and loneliness out there." Melinda gestures beyond the windows, which are clouded with steam. The Jewish contingent and Young Christians nod their heads. Yes, everybody knows how cold it is outside. But inside the radiators are clanging and sputtering. "My family doesn't understand me either, Arch," Melinda consoles. "I was the only one who wanted to travel, go to Russia."

People look a little nervous at that, shuffle their feet.

"Not Russia especially," Melinda amends. "Just away." She makes her hands look like birds on the wing. "Though I *was* arrested once. Voluntarily. I was protesting."

"Who would want to get arrested?" Arch asks.

"It was the least I could do, Arch."

"We only offer decaffinated." Charlene hands Leslie a cup of coffee. Everybody is seated at the tables now, drinking their soup and coffee, licking their pâté off Ritz crackers. The TV has been turned off, and an old Beatles song wafts in from the kitchen.

"I don't like the way Gary is looking," Melinda whispers to Charlene.

"Me neither. He's drunk out of his head."

"I remember when John Lennon died," Archie muses, shaking his head. "I nearly died myself. Bob Dylan is my second favorite. I don't know what I'm going to do when he dies."

"They treat you like kings here," Manny wants Leslie to know. "Put that in your show. Decaffinated, patties. What the hell is this stuff you spread on the crackers, Melinda, mud?"

"Some high-class goose liver, Manny, from a caterer."

"That reminds me of when I worked in a chicken factory," Manny remembers.

"Make it snappy, Manny. It's going to be lights-out in a minute. Gary, why don't you trot on over to the bathroom now before the rush?"

"Why does Gary look so funny, Charlene?"

"He's drunk and mad, Arch. Angry mad, not mad mad."

"As I was saying, factory is a glorification if I ever heard it, and the reason they called it that was the conveyor belts, one waist-high, the chickens chugging down in wooden crates, the other conveyor belt above dangling the not-quite-dead chickens. You were supposed to grab the chickens out of the crate real quick and hook their scrawny feet to the conveyor belt overhead. Only as soon as those poor suckers saw what was coming, they'd start shitting and squawking all over the place. Flying chicken shit is powerfully pungent, and I'm talking about your eyes squinted shut. Not only that, but what was flipping by overhead from the guys in front of you on the line was hardly what I would call nicely whole birds. Parts and pieces of parts — a leg dripping warm blood, a head, feathers matted like old tired rain."

"That was beautiful, Manny."

"You think so, Melinda?"

"We are going to have to edit," Leslie confides to Maury, "like seriously edit. Everybody and their two cents. I bet half of these stories are lies."

"I was a schoolteacher," Archie wants them to know.

"Is that where you kissed the elbows and knees of the teen-ager?"

"That happened at Dunkin' Donuts under the No Loitering Sign, my luck."

"I come from a long line of schoolteachers myself, and taught by a dutiful lady teacher hardly older than myself, our books handed down from the white school across town, and those teachers pressed their hair and tightened their lips and lifted every voice and sang."

"Thank you, Manny. It is now lights-out." Charlene rose from her chair. The volunteers had been busy setting up the cots in the middle of the room and cleaning out the kitchen.

"Where is Gary?" Melinda looks around the room.

"He's in the kitchen," Archie says.

"Out of the kitchen, Gar. Countdown time."

"One night I was in the bathtub listening to Bob Dylan . . ."

"Arch . . ."

"And drinking a beer when my kid opens up the door and throws the damn cat right on my chest. I leapt out of the tub like a holy terror and stark-naked charged after the little fucker, running into every room of the house until I found him cowering behind the furnace. 'I surrender, Daddy, I surrender.' It made me think."

"Of what, Arch?" Manny was heading to his cot.

"Countdown to lights, folks." Charlene, large and lumpy, stood by the light switch. People were making their way to the bathroom, the cots.

"I had a dog, too. Ajax. As a pup he was put in the yard with a fence around it. Every day he jumped a little higher, and one day, Manny, he was gone. That made me think, too."

"You think too much."

"Just a few more shots, Charlene, and we'll go." Leslie got up from the table.

"You can't film in the dark." Charlene turned off one set of lights. "The signal, folks."

The Young Christians had drawn up some chairs in a circle for late-night Bible Study in the kitchen.

"Come along, Maury, let's get a group shot." Leslie pulled the cameraman by the chord into the large room where the volunteers were going around bed by bed, pulling covers over people, tucking flaps under chins.

"Don't shoot Gary," Melinda cautioned. "He's real touchy when he's drunk."

"Plus he's real old when he's old." Arch had his cot right next to the kitchen. He liked to read right before he slept and used the light from the Bible Study. The radio was turned so low it was only a glow and a hum.

"Nine, fellows. I'm on number nine. Going to eight. Heads down, Gary."

"I want a drink of water."

"Gar, it's bedtime." Archie pulled his shoes off. It looked like Manny was going to sleep in his earmuffs.

"Tell them to get the fucking camera out of my face."

"Okay, Gary, they're going."

"Yankee go home," Melinda said, "and you have a home to go to. This is ours."

But Maury and Leslie, not heeding a word, were tiptoing up on Gary.

"He's so great," Leslie was saying, "such the perfect lush."

"Get away from me, get away." Gary began to shadowbox the camera.

"Let me handle this, Charlene." Archie got up, went over to Gary's cot.

"Need any help, Arch?" Manny, who had substituted earplugs for his earmuffs, sat up in his cot. "What's going on?"

"Gary," Arch was saying, "Gary, nobody is going to hurt you here. Just relax. We'll get rid of them."

"You tell them, Arch," Charlene said.

"Listen, people." Arch stood up, approached the camera. "Don't they have a heart out in TV land?" he said, glaring straight into the lens.

"Look," Leslie screamed. "Behind you. He has a knife."

Archie spun around. Manny jumped up. All the guests raised themselves from their pillows, and the volunteers crowded against the doorway between the kitchen and the big room.

"Gary, give me the knife," Arch said. "Give your friend Archie the knife."

"No," Gary pouted, "I won't."

"Gary." Arch held out his hand. "The knife, Gar, before you hurt yourself."

"No."

"Give it to me, Gar. Please."

"No," and with two quick thrusts Gary drove the knife into Archie's chest.

"Oh." Everybody felt wounded, but it was Archie who fell to his knees, folded over, bent double, and had to use the cot for support. The knife clattered to the floor.

"You've hurt me, Gar, you've cut me."

"Happy?" Manny spat at the camera as he jumped over two cots to reach Archie.

"Oh God Almighty," Charlene wailed, and the others began running around like chickens with their heads cut off, the Young Christians, and the Jews, and Melinda. Leslie Untaker, anchorwoman, peed her pants.

"Oh Maury," she sobbed, "I'm so embarrassed."

"Call the ambulance," Manny commanded, "call the police. Arch is hurt bad." Manny knelt down beside Archie, straightened him out. "Arch baby, let me look at those cuts."

Archie's baby-blue suit and white turtleneck sweater began to ooze blood. Manny undid Archie's vest and lifted the shirt. Two wounds, red as lipstick, like dripping dabs of paint, and in the shape of fish kisses, gaped over Archie's left nipple.

"Is it bad, Manny?" Arch gasped.

"Naw, it ain't nothing. Compared to what I've seen, you are on a picnic." Manny gently pulled Arch's shirt back in place. "Charlene," he screamed. "Get the hell on that phone and tell the medics to get here with a doctor pronto."

"It's bad," Arch rasped, his breath coming and going.

"No, no, just a precaution. Cuts need bandages, man, no problem."

"Is this the hotline?" Charlene boomed over the phone. "Yes, it is an emergency. We have a man here who is cut in the heart, stabbed, hurt. Get the picture. Where? At the Shelter for the Homeless, Twenty-fifth and Mable, the corner of Twenty-fifth. Hurry up."

Charlene placed the receiver back on its hook, put her head against the wall, and for a few seconds the large, dingy room was silent.

"Dear God," she prayed. "*Help* us."

"It was an accident," Gary choked out. "I didn't mean to hurt him."

"Well, you did, and you are going to pay plenty," Charlene said.

"There are about a hundred witnesses to this heinous crime," Leslie Untaker confirmed.

"He didn't mean to," Arch cried, but he was having great difficulty breathing. His throat rattled like something was stuck, chunks of metal.

"Where the fuck is the ambulance, I'd like to know?" Manny was holding Arch up in his arms, and wiping the sweat off Arch's face. "Where is the help when you need it in this town? Ordinarily, the cops are crawling all over the place."

"Am I going to make it, Manny?" Arch's eyes seemed to have lost their shine, and his frizzy blond hair, usually a halo about his head, hung limp, defeated.

"You are going to make it. You are going to the hospital, though, and sleep in a nice clean bed, have some cute nurses taking your temp. 'Open those cheeks, lover boy.' Oh, the life of Riley is coming up for you."

Melinda brought a damp rag, placed it over Arch's forehead.

"God, that feels good," Arch whispered.

Manny gave her a look, leaned over, whispered in her ear.

"It's the air I'm worried about," he hissed, "the air in or coming in the chest cavity. I don't know why he's losing his breath."

"But I don't want to go to the hospital," Arch moaned.

"Hush, man, save your breath." Gary looked worried.

"It's not the blood. Where are those cops?"

"But I don't want to go to jail."

"It was an accident," Gary wailed.

"Somebody get out there on the street and wave down the ambulance," Manny said. "You," he pointed to Leslie, "go out and make yourself useful. Put on your fur coat. They'll stop for you. Be a damsel in a dress."

"Her dress is wet," Maury murmured.

"Here, she can wear my pants." Gary sat down on his cot, scooted off his pants. "You'll catch cold." He pushed his pants over to Leslie, wound a blanket around his waist.

"Very slick move, Gar, but it won't get you any time off."

"I know, Melinda," and Gary put his head in his hands, wept piteously.

"We need something airtight," Manny announced.

"I have bandages in the first-aid kit," Charlene offered.

"You have any Saran Wrap?"

"Around my sandwiches," Melinda said. "Mayonnaise on it."

"Bring it."

Melinda went into the kitchen, came back with a wad of sticky paper which she smoothed and flattened against her stomach.

"That's my girlfriend," Manny said to Archie. "To the rescue." He lifted Archie's shirt.

"Do you know that one time I was in jail," Arch said very softly, "and the guy sharing my cell, just a kid really, hooked himself up with bandages from around his leg, and he hung himself. He had to kneel to do it, and he was so quiet about it, I didn't wake up. Can you imagine somebody wanting to die that much?"

"Shush, Arch." Manny spread the paper over Arch's wounds. The circle of onlookers clapped.

"I'm not going to die, am I?"

"No, you are not, and that is final, Arch."

A siren sounded in the distance. Somebody said, "Praise the Lord."

The sound got louder, and in another minute they heard a car, two cars, come to a stop, some voices, and then Leslie and a cop, two medics rumbled down the stairs.

"He's over there," Charlene said. "Let them through."

"The cops," Arch squeaked. "I'm a dead duck, Manny."

"Easy does it, Arch."

The cop knelt down beside Manny, lifted Arch's shirt. The medics put the stretcher on the floor, peered over the cop's shoulder.

"Who put that stuff on his chest?" They looked from Archie up at the crowd.

"I did," Gary confessed, hobbling up with the blanket wrapped around his waist. "I cannot tell a lie. Am I going to jail?"

Manny cleared his throat.

"Manny did it," Melinda corrected, pointing to Manny.

"Not Hari-Krishna George Washington with his thinking cap on, but you? You?"

Manny gave the cop a steely stare. "Me."

"Maybe they can give you a medal, Manny."

"Medals I got, Melinda. It's a job I need."

Archie was slid on to the stretcher, hooked up with blood in his veins, oxygen up his nose, a clean sheet covering his body, a big blanket over everything.

"Can you drive?" the cop asked Manny, as they followed the stretcher up the stairs.

Manny looked to the left of him, to the right, behind. "Are you talking to me, officer?"

"Yes, I am talking to you. I need somebody to drive my car while I drive the ambulance and the two medics handle him in the back. We're a little shorthanded tonight, budget cuts."

"My license is expired, sir."

"Shit, man, drive my car."

"Can my fiancée come along?"

"Bring your mother, I care, but hustle, your buddy is in trouble."

Manny grabbed Melinda's hand, pulled her up the steps out to the sidewalk. Everybody else followed, too. The ambulance and police car were up on the curbs, their little round hats rotating red and yellow like noisemakers on New Year's Eve. A light snow had begun to fall and the sidewalk was sparkly, as if flecks of diamonds had been scattered like seed for spring.

"It's like Christmas," Charlene uttered softly.

The doors of the rescue truck were open and Arch pulled in. The cop got in front, tossed Manny the keys to the police car.

"Do I get to blow the siren?"

"Wait, wait," Charlene called out. "What about apprehending the criminal? It's the guy without his pants on."

Gary, standing a discreet distance from the crowd under the God Loves You sign, hung his head in shame.

"I'm sorry," he muttered. "Truly."

"I'll have to come back for him. Can you subdue him?"

"Am I deputized, like in the movies?" Charlene asked.

"*Ciao.*" Melinda waved out of the passenger side of the police car.

"You are all invited to the wedding," Manny confirmed, his arm extended in a blessing. "June."

The rescue-squad truck took off in a screech, wobbling a little, righting itself, going on, and Manny followed full-blast.

"It would really be dumb if Arch died after all of this," Melinda said, turning her head to look at them back there, huddled together on the sidewalk, blankets draped over shoulders, shoes off. The group, the gang.

"Where's your faith, Melinda?"

"In what?"

"In me. I said he is not going to die."

"How do you know?" She pulled back her hair, craned her head around to look him full in the face.

"I wasn't in Nam for nothing, believe me."

They roared along, kicking up the snow, and leaving the people on the sidewalk, the very few and far between, in the dust wondering what had happened, if they would get to read about it the next morning. The Kitty Kat Lounge blinked its pink neon tail on and off, and the adult-bookstore owners were chaining up their doors, calling it a night. A few ladies paced the corners, but business was down. It was winter, after all.

"This is the life," Manny said, careening along. "Maybe I missed my calling, Melinda, what do you think?"

"I think you're swell, Manny."

The rescue-squad truck swung into the emergency entrance.

"I think I can park this baby illegally." Manny beamed, coming to a stop.

"They are taking your friend up to the trauma suite," the cop said, leaning over the opened window. "If you guys want to wait to find out how he's doing, I'll drive you back."

Manny and Melinda got out of the police car and went into the hospital with the cop. Arch was sped before them, nurses running along his side, doctors appearing from out of nowhere. And then he was gone behind two swinging doors, which reverberated, stilled.

"He's going to be fine," Manny said.

They walked down the empty hall to the waiting room. There were a few people smoking cigarettes, a family hunched together, gray with fatigue, and a couple of ladies quietly weeping.

"I can see why hospitals give Arch the creeps," Manny said.

"Mind if I smoke?" Melinda collapsed in a chair, dug around in her army bag, pulled out a pack of Camels.

"I'm going for a cup of coffee in the cafeteria," the cop said. "You want?"

"Thank you." Manny reached into his pocket.

"On me. Milk, sugar?"

"The works," Manny answered, "for both my wife and me."

Melinda lit up, let out a long puff of smoke, inched down in her chair.

"A moment of truth," she said to Manny. "How did you get here, in this?"

"Same as you," Manny replied. "Of woman born. My friend is in the hospital."

"You know what I mean, Manny, don't evade the question."

"Oh, so you can tell the kids, huh, about their old man?"

"So *I* could know."

"Melinda, Melinda." He took her hand, held it up to the light.

"You did good tonight, Manny."

"Surprised?"

"A little."

"So you want to know who I am, where I came from, just like the TV lady. Well, see the earplugs I wear in my ears? Notice how I wear something over my ears all the time? Earmuffs, whatever? But I can hear everything. A pin drop over there, all the comings and goings. I hear, but just softer. Because, you know, I hate noise and glare, anything loud. Before the earmuffs, I wore a towel around my head and grew a big beard. That was when I was new to the street, you hear what I'm saying?"

"Yes, I do."

"Once, Melinda, standing in front of the Trailways, the hookers spattering like rain all around me clickity-click, you want to go on a date, honey, I saw somebody I used to know before I went overseas. I thought I might know the guy and he thought he knew me and he thought I knew him, and he looked at the towel wrapped around my head and my big, big beard, and he looked at how I looked, and he said, 'Hey, Manny, you got a toothache?' Melinda, I looked back hard at him. But he kept on. 'Hey, Manny,' he said. 'Is that you?' 'No,' I answered from behind my towel. 'It ain't me.' But it was, Melinda. It was and it is."

Everything You've Heard Is True

I am writing this from the madhouse, but I am not crazy. I am a political prisoner and I be here because they have no women's wing in the regular jail. If you want to talk about madness, it is not confined between these high, stone walls, but rather run riot on the island. Some say madness here long before Prime Minister Godfrey Simpson take over, that it always here—in the ground the goats eat and the babies dig at, and part of the banana skin they feed to the big, black pig tie up by the Holiday Inn. Some say crazy is part of our heritage from the Arawak and Carib Indians, the first people on Colinas. Maybe. Maybe so.

In the book of the Arawaks, told on their pots not by words but by pictures, Colinas and the other small islands were made when God dropped a calabash gourd from the sky and it break up into many small pieces. The other story is that bat mate with frog made the egg, which is the land. But the Arawaks died out long ago, long before the English came with the African slaves. The Arawak day lasted until the Caribs came on boat from the bigger islands with vengeance in their hearts and stone tomahawk in their hands. Cannibals. And rather than be conquered, killed, and eaten, all the Arawaks jumped off the highest cliff, the one on the east tip. Suicide Cliff they call it still, and have a little sign. We were here, it say, and now we gone. Not in those words, of course.

Do you think I think of suicide myself? Me, Mrs. Sweet, Althea Sweet? I think, yes, but would never do, not only because it is a sin, the sin of despair, but because I am praying, praying for a helicopter, a big American dragonfly that will let down its rope ladder in the middle of the madhouse yard and take me up with it into the sky, make a giant shadow on the green hills and over the beaches, over boys with donkeys and women carrying heavy baskets on their head down to market in town, over the Prime Minister's mansion and out to open sea. It would not be the CIA helicopter, for we know who they like and where they be, but friends of the Peace Corps workers. Even if it be from Castro's Cuba, that be okay with me. Perhaps I am crazy to believe in this metal angel, but I do, every night. Every night, I listen hard. And even when morning come, I do not give up, looking up all day long from the rock where I sit.

The wall that goes around the madhouse garden is made of rocks and concrete, no chinks in between, and maybe it is about twelve feet high. On the top of the wall, planted like flowers, is a row of broken glass, bit pieces which shine in the sun like razors. I am not the only one who studies that wall. There is a girl here who watches at the wall while she talks to God. God say I be going home soon, she tell me in the morning. That's nice, dear. What can I say? I wish God would whisper in my ear and I don't mean nothing nasty either. Then there is the old lady who wear a chameleon around her neck, only it ain't changing color anymore. Just skin and bones, really. It was a pet and it died. At least, I say to myself, it not an iguana. Which they have in the tall bush by the back wall.

My main friend here is a man they keep strapped down on a table. The rest of us sleep in the hammocks they string up every night on the open porch between the two buildings. Mr. B.'s problem is that he cannot keep his hands off himself. And even strapped down it peak up, I mean, no hands, just the thought enough. This big bamboo, he say to me with great sadness in his voice, it have its own mind. I am the one who feeds him. The thing wave at me, but Mr. B. means no harm. What can he do?

Now there are others, too. The place plenty fill up, no vacancy at the madhouse, but I must say that I am the person of consequence here. At one time I had the only real-estate license on the island, granted to me by the Prime Minister for certain services rendered. This is before he go mad with power, and spies and traitors spring up like grass in the soccer field after rain, this is before he take away the waters from the fisherman, the land from the farmer and all the business along the bay, including the Turtleback restaurant, in my family for twenty-five years. All belong to him. When the Americans come on the tourist boat, it is he who makes the duty. Little naked boys dive for pennies. When the American medical school start up, who puts out his hand for bribe? Meanwhile all our rents go up. The taxi fleet? The goats and cows? Hotels? The radio station, Radio Antilles-Colinas? Now they read out the people who got their electricity turn off. So? Let them read. People like to hear their name on the radio. Only the newspaper remain free and that a stop-and-go proposition, every issue.

People complain. Sure. But not too loud. Bad-mouthing the P.M. will go on forever. That is life. Because for there to be action, injustice must come and sit at your kitchen table. It has to come home with you. And that is what happen to me.

The darkness and heat were as thick as blood pudding that night, and the moon was full and a sick gray color. My son—his son, for who could know who was not the P.M.'s son in those days—was sitting at the kitchen table drinking white rum. White rum and coconut juice, a little ice, a little lime. My machete for cracking coconuts open was standing there by the table.

I remember seeing the hibiscus bush out the window, the flower trumpets closed up for the night. I remember the sound of my tap dripping. I remember the little mosquito netting cover I had placed over my cut mango. The last thing my son said was, Why you do that to me, Daddy. Why?

At the trial the P.M. say it accident and white rum, accident and a white-hot rage. Well, the judge and jury were his. The police belong to him and I could not hire a lawyer who was not in this pay. No surprise at finding that cutting open his son's head with a machete was accident. Accident. For years I seething accident, each moment I marking my time, watching, waiting. I play the game, smile, keep my real-estate license, act like friend to him, put flowers on my son's grave. Accident? I show him accident is what I thinking. But I had no plan until they came to me, ask me to help.

Before Bouncey drive a cab, he one of the people who live on the beach, make basket and such for the Americans and Germans who come to walk naked in our country. Bouncey make basket, hat, sell a little *ganga*, run the hermit-crab races over at the Holiday Inn on Thursday nights and sometimes, and this is what they do, pair up with some lonely American person. Male or female, they ain't care. Two weeks, some nice meals, and the big picture is somebody to sponsor them, brother, sister, take me to America, Daddy. All this going on when Bouncey's brother die. Under mysterious circumstance.

There is a little more to it than that. Bouncey's brother one of the people who take to the hills to fight, hide, hide and fight. They call themselves the Maroons after the Jamaican slaves who long time ago say *N-O* to their masters. The Colinian Maroons do the same, and some got guns. From Cuba? Who knows, who cares? I think they are smuggled in from the States. Magnums like in the movie with Charles Bronson. But the story is that there is a corpse over at the medical-school anatomy laboratory which is Colinian, a Colinas man, and some say it is Bouncey's brother.

The medical school, if you are wondering, is in the Old Four Seasons Hotel on the west by the beach, and the anatomy laboratory is in the old ballroom. No Colinian will let himself end up there, no sir. All bodies are claimed these days and they always were, so they have to import bodies for cutup from Florida, which come on Palmair cargo holds. The plane come on Saturdays.

The thing is this corpse is different, the cleanup lady tell everybody. The feet. The feet not used to shoes. Even poor Americans wear shoes from the time they can walk. And the teeth. They be rotten. Now even poor Americans drink milk when they be young. The face is ruined, so they can't tell for sure who it is, but the skin and body be from here. We, in Colinas, be quite black. Not a mixture like the Trinidadians, who go with Calcutta Indians and the Chinese. We mostly African, because the first Indians all killed out. Yes, the English got those fierce Caribs. And no coolie Indian or Chinese brought in extra. Just slaves and English. So soon cousins marrying cousins, and we are all very black except for a few. Me, for instance I am light. And Linton Fitzroy, the schoolmaster, and the P.M. himself. Anyway, Bouncey sneak in, can tell it *is* his brother, and smuggle him out, give him proper Shango burial, and from there Bouncey learn to drive, get permission and money for a cab. How, we don't know. He was in training, he told us, to be the P.M.'s chauffeur. Very interesting, Linton Fitzroy say. Linton talks like that because he is head schoolmaster at Colinas Boys' Secondary. What the P.M. don't know (and I think it strange the P.M., with all his spies, don't know) is that Bouncey was planning to drive the P.M. right off a cliff. Guess which one? But now that is not necessary, Linton say. And no Shango spells necessary either. For he has a plan.

By the way, the P.M. practice Shango, too. And he Rosicrucian, tomb of the ages. I mean, that man leave no stone unturned. He is the one who put the cross up on the highest hill to scare away the UFOs. It is to keep the jumbies from walking backward on Judgment Day, some nonsense like that. People say his power come from the Shango he practice. People say he walk right out of the bush to become P.M. True enough, he come from the bush, from a tiny village where there just be women and children. All the men gone to town, St. Catherine, the capital of Colinas. The P.M., Linton Fitzroy and Father Benedict, defrocked and in disgrace now and before the assassination attempt, all come from that little village of all women. See, things go back far. They came to go to Colinas Boys' Secondary, little boys in short pants. And they call themselves the Three Musketeers. They learn French, how to do hard sums, and have their picture taken in their school tie and blazer. Father Benedict then go to the States to study, get radical after Vatican II. He believe and said in the pulpit (which is why he was taken off by the P.M.'s police, his church locked against him), he say that Jesus the first Communist. Fitzroy went to Canada to the university and the P.M. went to Jamaica, U.W.I., at Mona.

Linton Fitzroy and the P.M., it said, have the same father. Fitzroy told me he did not know his father, but he knew *who* he was. Clear to see his father not from Colinas. A Trinidadian, originally Calcutta Indian, who sold cloth from a suitcase, his father went around village to village right before the rainy season. Linton and the P.M. born within a week of each other. And they raised like brothers in truth, so that when the P.M. came to power, Linton Fitzroy was counting on Minister of Education, at the very least. Instead the P.M. choose out of the pack of the police one Honor McIntire, a man who I wonder if he can read. The whole cabinet come from the police force, for we have no army. And why were we surprised? History is history.

It was 1976 and nobody born yesterday when it all happen. The P.M. a country schoolteacher then. Nobody expected him to be leading the Sugarcane Worker Union down the hills, all roads leading into St. Catherine clogged with workers, their machetes raised to the sky, the P.M. at the end on a white horse. On strike, on strike, they shout. And next it was the plantation workers. For weeks we did not hear the trucks rumbling down from the hills early in the morning when it is still dark and the road is wet and slick. The bananas come from the interior to the United Fruit Boat on the dock, the little boys riding like pashas on top of the stacked stalks. No. Let them rot, let them rot.

The Reynolds Bauxite Mine had to close down, too. Nothing move in or out. The sewing factory they have set up on the dock under the canvas they have stretched on what look like the bones of a whale, that get quiet, all the women go home. The Friday-morning tourist boat must make a big detour. I'm telling you, it was something. Independence Day. The P.M.-to-be on white horse.

When the English left, they couldn't get out fast enough. Running lickety-split in their white linen suits, they tripped over their silver tea sets, let the ice melt in their gin and tonics, and, on their verandas facing the sea, you could pick up books, *Wild Flowers of the Caribbean*, the pages flipped open in the afternoon breeze.

The P.M. said, and won his election no trouble with, these words: I born here like you, educated at Colinas Boys' Secondary, went to the university only a few islands away. I marry a good Colinas woman. [No comment on that, the poor lady.] I one of you, and Colinas be our country.

I remember, dear heart, going to town on the minibus shortly after that, those days of speechmaking and marching around with the new flag of three green hills on a field of stars. I remember passing the old people's home, seeing the goats sleeping on the mounds of the old people's graveyard in the back of their home, passing the Planned Parenthood building with the women in a line wrapping around the yard, men on the bus shouting out, Get fix up for me, darling, I coming by tonight. I remember seeing the icehouse and yacht club and the hotels and the beaches and a man on a bicycle carrying a full load of green bananas on his head. I remember seeing the women squatting by their wares at the marketplace, holding umbrella against the hot sun, the brick church, and even looking up at the madhouse on the hill. I remember seeing all that like it all new. All new and it belong to me. My country, my place. I was so proud.

Manfred, the lighthouse keeper, another person in on our plot, tell me the same with him. He was so proud. That was before he ask for the investigation of the medical school and got lighthouse arrest, which is naturally where we have to meet, driving out at night, picking up Father Benedict at his former church, where he still was sleeping, sneaking in through a tunnel that he says there since the Arawaks, but everybody else knows the secret catacomb made by the Christian

Brothers to keep wine in. Bouncey drive his cab is how we go as if to party—Father Benedict in the front, Linton and me in the back, and of course Manfred waiting for us at the lighthouse.

In the dark we pass the old, broken Landrover left behind by the English marked in black letters, U.K. Rabies Control, and the two cypress trees on the Atlantic side, their branches pushed back by the wind like women's hair, Manfred's clothesline with his two pants flapping like sea gulls, and we go into his small concrete house, sit on his metal bunk, everything dark except the lantern, which show our faces, the Colman stove, his picture of Fidel Castro torn out of *Life*. This is how it's going to be, Linton starts out, and we lean forward, our voices hushed and our very breath catching in our throats. This is how it's going to be:

Easter Sunday, the regatta and blessing of the fleet. There is always a little parade of boats going around the harbor blowing their horns, tooting their whistles. The lead boat always have the most important people. Since 1976, that means it is always the P.M., his ministers, and lately a Japan man in a three-piece suit, soon to start a shrimp factory on the wharf, the Peace Corps head come from Barbados, the president of the American medical school, some favorite women, and Father Donovan, who take over from Father Benedict. And me. Yes, I am important people. Still, at that time. Remember, I playing game, breathing, thinking, living: accident.

While we talk I am looking up at the three flights of metal stairs which lead up to the lighthouse. Three flights and then a small ladder, a ledge ringing a cylinder of glass. The lighthouse light itself is glass over glass, stripes of carved glass, ribbons of glass woven over each other like snakes biting each other's tails, and at the heart of this layers of glass is the giant wick. Yes, kerosene wick, who needs electricity? Manfred got to keep the monster fed, though, all night long, and the whole thing have to move to the left and very slow, back to the right, to the left, and to the right, on a turnstile Manfred must crank up every ninety minutes.

You are going to be on that boat, the lead boat, Linton Fitzroy tells me that night, his face as fierce in the half-light of the lantern as a hunter shooting for manicou in the night forest. You and everybody and their champagne glass on a small yacht, crowded, back to back, on the *Bonnie Doom*.

The name of the boat is *Bonnie Dune*, and it left by the English

Governor, one of the things he didn't have time to take, sell, or give away.

Just a little shove, Linton say, a little push, a little bump, a little oops, excuse me.

The thing is, the P.M. can't swim. I can't either, but I always wear a life jacket if even I three feet in sight of the water. There be plenty people who cannot swim. It is a well-kept secret.

Linton and Benedict, three hundred pounds, plan to be under the boat, in scuba suits, helping nature on its way. A little tug at the legs is all. The rest take care of itself. Free elections and so forth. They plan to go to Trinidad for Carnival, happen to pick up some suits and air tanks.

Well, the night before Easter, and I am nervous. I hear the lizards scratching over the tin roof and nearly jump out of *my* skin. It not do to stay home, anyway, because there is a big party for visiting guests at the P.M.'s nightclub, the Midnight Castle. So I go.

All his women, and he have a few, are hostesses in long dresses the colors of flowers, poinsettia-red and fuchsia-purple and hibiscus-orange. They swish back and forth bringing the food to a long table near the back. The place done up in Christmas lights although it Easter, and Lent at that, with gold framed mirrors and black iron furniture in the shape of leaves and flowers, and plenty of white cloth, curtains and tablecloths. Like you in heaven. And if you still in doubt, the food convince you for sure. Tannia soup, breadfruit and callaloo soup, lambi chowder, curried lobster, broiled dolphin, swordfish, turtle meat, tuna, shark, crab cake and shrimp, blood pudding, manicou, and cristophene, green fig, yams, fried plantain, stewed chicken, goat, rice and pigeon peas, rice and red beans, macaroni pie, white hops bread, New Zealand butter, Dutch cheese, ginger beer, sorrel, papaya, dasheen, zabocca, and mango ice cream. And I sitting there thinking, God help me, that the boat be heavy tomorrow, the heavier the better.

So the day come. I watch the sun come up over the sea, the people in the shanties on the hill come out and go down the hill to the standpipe for water. I hear the animals in the zoo wake up, and imagine all the plants in the botanic gardens below the P.M.'s pink mansion unfurling their leaves. The day is born. The police band begin practicing over at the police barracks, and the blue of the harbor like poured-on blue, flat and smooth, no ripple, nothing to hint trouble. It is, I think like a book, a perfect day for murder.

At first, when I am on the boat, I do not see Manfred's boat. The plan is that Linton and the Father, on board Manfred's boat, will row around the peninsula. They will drop in from a distance, swim underneath to where we suppose to be. It is a foolproof plan. Fifteen minutes out of dock, giving Linton and the Father time to be under the main boat, I am supposed to be next to the P.M., doing my thing. I look back at the boats behind us, try to spot Bouncey. He drove me out. I see Bouncey. He gives me a little nod. When I look out again, I see Manfred's boat. Only Manfred in it, meaning that Linton and the Father are already streaming toward us.

Out we chug. Everybody on the *Bonnie Dune* is already quite drunk. Champagne glasses, the plastic kind, thrown overboard, bob on top of the water. Things seem a little confused. The police band has started to play a hymn calypso beat and some are trying to dance on the boats. Good, I think, just fine. Meantime, the Father and Linton getting closer, closer, quietly, secretly. I feel strange, like there is a big clock somewhere, and it is sounding loud, tolling. I am sticking close to the P.M., quite close. I give him a little bump. Oops, excuse me. He looks at me, walks on to the other side of the boat. Then it is time. I move up against him. My hip is what does it. Man overboard, somebody shouts. The P.M. is overboard. The P.M. is flailing around, splashing. He is on top of the water, underneath. He comes up once. A bodyguard has thrown him a life preserver, but he can't reach it. The P.M. goes under again, and this time he does not come up. There is a shout on board. Who can swim? A woman dives in, a man. A bunch of people in the water now.

I can't explain it, but I begin to scream. I scream out, Save him, save him. And I mean it. I really mean it. And something happens under the water because I see the Father and Linton Fitzroy in their scuba suits hoisting the P.M. up. I see Manfred rowing in close. Bouncey is shouting, too. We are all the same. We want him saved. The P.M. is pulled up on the boat. Linton follows behind him. It take three men to haul up the Father. Then they have the P.M. on the deck, stretched out like a dead fish. But Linton does not give up. He begins working over him lip-to-lip, cheek-to-cheek. No, let me, the Father say, reaching for the P.M's chest with his huge hands, down, up, down and up. By then Bouncey and Manfred have gotten on board. We, our group, make a little circle around the wet body. The Father and Linton are in their wet suits. I realize it is all very suspicious. I was about to say something, offer a little suggestion. Just then the P.M. opens his eyes, coughs up some water and champagne. P.M., are you okay? Manfred asks. The P.M. blinks. Bouncey hold his head up for him. The P.M. looks from Linton to the Father, who resembles a slippery, black dolphin, man's friend, not a demon of the deep. From the Father, the P.M's eyes go to Manfred, then me. He take a good, hard look at me, turns around to Bouncey. You, too, the P.M. says to Bouncey. Then he shakes his head. I think maybe he is going to smile, laugh, call it even. Instead, he command, Arrest them, the lot for treason against the state.

And so it happen. Just like that. When it came down to it, we didn't have what it take. No killer instinct, as they say. We simply could not do it, couldn't kill the man. Instead we save him. But to us it doesn't make any difference that in the long-run we save him, for he puts us in jail, me in the madhouse. We should have killed him, right? But we cannot go back and, even if we go back to a minute before, I know it would turn out the same.

At night here at the madhouse, I have dreams. I dream of the airport, the way it is in December, the runway banked with poinsettia bushes, more red than green, "Joy to the World" on the steel drum broadcast over the runway so some silly Americans can dance until the plane comes in. I dream of the old blind lady who sit on the airport porch selling green oranges from a basket. Oranges, sweet oranges, she sing to the empty sky. No lights at the airport, you know, so the plane must always come and go in the day, and only small Palmair planes, old Rolls-Royce engines, for the runway end sharply on the beach. In the waiting room they have two photos, one is the P.M. He, as always, is in white. White riding pants in this picture, black boots, the whip. Like he English or something. The other picture is of Miss Colinas, who went on to become Miss World, my mother. She is in a white bathing suit. This is before me, before my father, who was one of the English who drop in for more than tea and had something urgent to see about in England ten years later, like he left the pot on to boil.

At night here in the madhouse, out on the porch, in my hammock, I can study the stars good. In Colinas you are close to the stars and far away from everything else. The overseas edition of *Time* on the coffee table in the Holiday Inn is about three months old. Sometimes during these nights looking up at the stars, I think that maybe Colinas not an island in the Caribbean Sea, but a small planet in the sky. So that it would have to be a spaceship who save me, not American helicopter. Maybe, I think, it will have to be God himself who save me.

Frances Sherwood's stories have appeared in *California Quarterly, Literary Review, Playgirl,* and elsewhere. She is a member of the English Department at Indiana University, South Bend.

Everything You've Heard Is True

Designed by Ann Walston.

Composed by Capitol Communication Systems, Inc., in Sabon text and Kaufman display type.

Printed by R. R. Donnelley and Sons Company on 55-lb. S. D. Warren's Cream White Sebago, and bound in Holliston Aqualite with Lindenmeyr Elephant Hide endsheets.